IMPROPER CONDUCT

Misbehaviour at Work
A Mischief Collection of Erotica

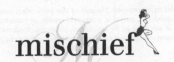

mischief

Mischief
An imprint of HarperCollins*Publishers*
77–85 Fulham Palace Road,
Hammersmith, London W6 8JB

www.mischiefbooks.com

A Paperback Original 2013

First published in Great Britain in ebook format by
HarperCollins*Publishers* 2012

Copyright
Model Employee © Donna George Storey
Lather. Rinse. Repeat. © Lolita Lopez
Work It © Heather Towne
Peaches © Lizzie Behan
Military Police © Georgie Taylor
Between The Covers © Elizabeth Coldwell
Bodies © Lux Zakari
The Invisible Woman © Amber Leigh
In Your Dreams © Chrissie Bentley
Stud Farm © Deva Shore

The author asserts the moral right to
be identified as the author of this work

A catalogue record for this book is
available from the British Library

ISBN-13: 9780007553167

Find out more about HarperCollins and the environment at
www.harpercollins.co.uk/green

CONTENTS

Model Employee
Donna George Storey   1

Lather. Rinse. Repeat.
Lolita Lopez   19

Work It
Heather Towne   36

Peaches
Lizzie Behan   55

Military Police
Georgie Taylor   76

Between The Covers
Elizabeth Coldwell   91

Bodies
Lux Zakari   108

The Invisible Woman
Amber Leigh   131

In Your Dreams
Chrissie Bentley   149

Stud Farm
Deva Shore   166

Model Employee
Donna George Storey

Thirty minutes. That's all the time she had until the meeting began. Zara took the stairs two at a time, but stopped to collect herself before she pushed open the door to the fourth floor. Officially this wing of the building was not in use by her company, but the clever planning that served her well in her career was equally useful for this particular action item.

Chin held high, she strode into the hallway. If she happened to meet anyone, she would confidently claim she was on her way to the CEO's office to discuss her upcoming presentation. Yet, in the six months she'd been engaging in this special 'preparation' for important staff meetings, she'd never met a soul.

With one final glance down the empty corridor, she slipped into the WC by the stairwell and locked the door behind her. It might seem strange to make a special trip

1

upstairs to answer the call of nature, to put it one way, but Zara was partial to this particular room. It was of an intimate size, with a sink, a single stall and a lounging bed upholstered in fake leather. The lighting was unusually flattering thanks to the sconces around the mirrors, and the air always had the fresh scent of lemony disinfectant cleaner. Zara suspected it was rarely used, except by her for this very special purpose.

She hung her purse and suit jacket on the hook by the sink and turned to study herself in the full-length mirror. She looked a little tired, she thought, although she was pleased with her new haircut that just grazed her jawline. Sophisticated it was, the perfect look for a vice president of marketing. She gave herself a sly smile. She had twenty-eight minutes now.

Still gazing at her reflection, she began to unbutton her blouse. She pulled it slightly down over her shoulders and unsnapped her white satin bra by its front hook. The cups parted and her breasts spilled out, as if eager to escape their workaday bondage. Her nipples were already stiff and rosy.

Her secret muscles clenched with anticipation, and she bit her lip to keep from moaning. If only the company elites could gather here instead of the conference room on the floor below. What would they say to see her like this, breasts exposed, chest splotched with sexual rash, eyes hooded with lust?

'My model employee,' Michael Jones, the CEO, would tell her. He always said this in a slightly flirtatious tone, but he did in fact seem pleased with her work.

But now she was of a mind to model a different professional behaviour – the kind you find in a red-light district. Zara took her breasts in her hands and began to massage them lightly, half for her own pleasure, half for the show on display in the silvery world receding before her.

'Oh, my God, I can't believe it. She's standing there playing with her bare tits in front of everyone,' a husky male voice murmured in her ear.

'You're going to enjoy this week's presentation,' promised another, sounding very much like the CEO.

'Pardon me, sir, but what might we expect on today's agenda?'

'First Ms Reynolds will masturbate for us until she comes. If we've shown her our appreciation with plenty of lewd comments, she'll choose one lucky man to bang her on the conference table until she climaxes again.'

'Choose me, darling, I'll give your cunt a good ploughing.'

Zara pinched her nipples, twisting the hard nubs between her fingers. She didn't need to answer. She didn't even really know who these phantom men were, but their crude words aroused her like nothing else.

'Lovely breasts, but why don't you show us your bare bottom and your pretty lady parts as well?'

Obligingly Zara unzipped and let her wool pants slither down around her knees. She yanked her satin panties down and spread her thighs as if to show herself to a roomful of voyeurs.

'There's a quim I'd like to get to know better.'

'Touch it, sweetheart. Touch your hard clit. That's what we're here to see.'

Zara dropped one hand between her legs and pressed a finger to her sweet spot.

'Suggestible, isn't she, boss?'

'She's my model employee,' observed the CEO.

Zara hastily glanced at her watch. Five minutes had passed. She began to strum herself industriously, aware of the soft click of her lubricated flesh.

'I love to watch that finger jiggle, but you're running out of time. I think you need the help of your special "friend".'

Unfortunately the man was right. Zara did have a tight schedule today. She waddled over to her purse as best she could with her pants around her knees and fished out her treasure. She pulled the egg-shaped vibrator from its case and switched it on. It cost over a hundred dollars and was advertised to be absolutely quiet. It was indeed – except for the gasps that leaked from her lips when she held the shivering tip to her clitoris.

Again she faced the mirror. She licked her palm and brushed it over her nipple in slow circles. With the other hand, she held the toy to her mons.

4

'Oh, sweet Jesus!' That was Zara's voice, hissing out her pleasure when the vibrator made contact.

'She'll come like a rocket and then one of us will have her,' said a voice. 'It doesn't take her long to come again with a cock buried inside her.'

A hazy veil of lust dropped over Zara's eyes, but she kept her gaze fixed on the female body before her. The woman in the mirror was so sexually aroused that her breasts were mottled with a pink flush, her thighs were shaking and her ass bucked up as if the vibrator were a man's groin. The burning sensation around her clit expanded, pushing up into her belly like a balloon. With wild eyes, she glanced down at her watch on her left wrist. Thirteen minutes until the meeting began.

She pressed the toy deeper into her flesh.

And came.

Zara squeezed her eyes shut, lost in the searingly pleasurable sensation pulsing through her body. When the last spasm subsided, she opened her eyes again and flashed herself another smile. But she had no time to waste. She immediately hiked up her slacks and fastened her bra and blouse. She dabbed her face with a handkerchief, applied fresh lipstick, and brushed out her hair. There was nothing like an orgasm to improve one's appearance.

'Why's she leaving? Didn't you say one of us gets to fuck her now?'

'Maybe next time, if you're good,' Zara murmured

under her breath. Poor lad, trapped in the mirror with a throbbing hard-on. Didn't he know not to trust any promises a woman made *before*, when she'd tell a man anything to get what she needed for her release?

She was still smiling at her own joke as she pushed open the ladies' room door.

And nearly ran right into a man passing by.

'Oh, pardon me,' she cried.

'No, pardon me,' he said, equally surprised at her sudden appearance out of nowhere.

Zara noted that the man had a pleasantly deep voice. She instinctively looked up into his face. He wasn't bad looking either, rather her type with his square face and intelligent blue eyes, not to mention the stocky body type she favoured in her men. More to wrap your legs around.

'I didn't know there were any offices in use up here,' he said.

'Oh, there aren't, I was just coming back from a meeting with the CEO, and now I'm off to another meeting,' Zara babbled. Not that she owed a visitor any explanations.

The man cocked his head. 'I was just with your CEO for the past hour. And now I'm going to the weekly executive status meeting on the third floor. Is that where you're headed?'

Caught in her lie, Zara's cheeks turned to flame. 'Yes, actually. I'm afraid I didn't realise we'd have guests at the meeting today.'

To her relief, the man only smiled and began walking toward the stairwell. She followed.

'I'm not exactly a guest. I'm a consultant. Michael asked me in to evaluate the company's current organisation.'

Zara frowned. That kind of consultant often meant someone lost her job or was transferred to the Siberia of 'special projects'.

The man seemed to read her thoughts. 'I don't think there's anything to worry about. We're talking fine tuning here. By the way, I'm Paul Springfield, principal with Springfield Management Training.' He held out his hand.

'Zara Reynolds. VP of marketing.'

Paul's eyebrows shot up. 'Zara Reynolds? What a coincidence. Michael was just telling me to pay special attention to you. He said you give the best damn presentations in the company.'

Could it be that at the very moment she was practising her private warm-up exercise, Michael and this stranger were discussing her charisma before an audience?

'I don't mean to put you on the spot. Your boss is just very impressed with you,' Paul said. This man certainly seemed considerate, if nothing else. 'By the way, I'm glad to see you like to get your blood pumping during the workday.'

Again she was speechless. It was as if he *knew* what she'd been doing.

'I also try to take the stairs instead of the elevator for

exercise whenever I can,' he continued innocently and set off at a brisk pace down the stairway.

In spite of herself, Zara joined him, although she would have preferred to disappear into the woodwork. Still, if her boss and this intriguing outsider were expecting her to perform well at the meeting, she would not disappoint them.

***

Zara's presentation did go very well. Once in the conference room, she quickly recovered the easy confidence she always felt after a good orgasm. Far from throwing her off her game, Paul's sky-blue eyes provided an extra spark. In fact, her entire audience seemed captivated by her report, laughing freely at her jokes, nodding enthusiastic agreement at her suggestions.

'They were right about you,' Paul murmured as she brushed past him on her way out.

She just smiled.

She found herself smiling at Paul often over the next month of his consultant work. They ran into each other daily on the stairways, and both favoured the organic vegetarian restaurant near the office. Over lunch one day, he let it be known that he'd been divorced for a few years. She mentioned the relationship she'd ended when she moved to the city to take this job. Halfway through

8

his project, Paul confessed he'd love to take her out to his favourite upscale vegetarian restaurant for dinner, but he made it a policy never to mix business with pleasure. Might she have a free evening after he'd turned in his final evaluation?

Zara's smile promised more than dinner. After all, she'd already been indulging herself in scandalous behaviour with Paul during her breaks in her special hideaway. She still performed for her colleagues, but Paul took on the role of emcee now. His satin voice narrated each new move in obscene language; his large hands and hot mouth demonstrated particularly effective techniques to heighten her response. When she was feeling really naughty, Paul would whip out a fat, florid erection and instruct her to fellate him while he leaned back against the conference table. He always pulled out just in time to ejaculate pearly spunk all over her face for the edification of her watching co-workers.

The climaxes she had from these lascivious scenes were fabulous.

Soon after he finished his work with her company, Paul did ask her to dinner, and soon after that, they went to bed together. She was not disappointed. The first night had a leisurely, innocent festivity, as if they were teenagers discovering sex for the first time. Once he realised she was adventurous, however, he revealed his true nature as a sexual connoisseur. He introduced her to his collection of special pillows to facilitate unusual sexual positions – wedges and bolsters and rockers, which he covered in washable satin cases – and draped her body over them in the most stimulating ways.

Unbeknownst to him, he also became bolder at the imaginary company meetings, urging her to masturbate shamelessly with a long, veined dildo and bending her over the table and sodomising her in front of the assembled employees to the surprise and delight of all. Nothing made her hotter than these forbidden scenes, which she sometimes played in her head as they made love, but she still wasn't sure the real Paul would be able to handle her transgressive use of office hours. After all, his first impression of her was as a model employee.

That changed one day when they were enjoying brunch at the corner table in their favourite café after a Saturday morning of sweaty sex involving a pair of lacy crotchless knickers (hers) and multiple configurations of sex pillows (his). Over tofu scrambles, Paul took Zara's hand across the table and gazed into her eyes.

'You look so gorgeous right now. But then you've always looked radiant to me from the first moment I laid eyes on you.'

Zara laughed indulgently.

'I figured you'd been making yourself up in that ladies' room. But now I know it's just your natural beauty. You have a glow every time we're together.'

If only he knew.

'I always wondered, though ...'

'Yes?'

'Well, I was wondering why you were in that deserted part of the building. I'm guessing that room has good lighting for make-up. Or you like to have a bit of exercise.'

'Well, you're right on both counts, but not for the reason you think.' The words slipped out before Zara could stop herself. Then she blushed. Paul looked even more intrigued.

'Come on, what's up? I insist you tell me.'

Zara's pussy contracted. She loved to submit to his commands when it came to sex, and this was unquestionably about sex. So she scooted her chair closer and brought her lips to his ear. 'I do something, well, unprofessional in that room.'

He grinned. 'What do you mean? Like you make calls to other companies to divulge secrets?'

'Of course not.' She leaned close again. 'I "relax" myself when I'm feeling stressed. You know, with that toy I showed you the other night.'

Paul's jaw dropped. 'You mean when we first met you'd just been ...? No wonder I fell for you at first sight.'

To Zara's relief, he seemed far from appalled by her confession.

'I want details. Come on, you can tell me all about it in the car.'

11

Once they were out of public hearing, she slowly divulged the basic facts: that she sneaked up to the deserted ladies' room and pretended she was giving a sex show to her co-workers while she masturbated. She did not, however, mention the disembodied male voices or Paul's own enthusiastic participation in the depravity. She was so caught up in her story, she didn't notice he was driving them to her office until they'd parked in front of the building. She knew Paul well enough to guess what he had in mind.

'What if we get caught?' she asked helplessly.

'It's a Saturday,' he insisted. 'No one will be there. If they are, you can say you stopped in to pick up some work. You're well known for your dedication to the company.'

Part of her wanted to refuse, but the tingling between her legs told her that she'd regret it.

'OK, I'll give you a peek at the scene of the crime, but that's all.'

Paul gave her a 'we'll see' smile and jumped out of the car.

He suggested they take the stairs, for authenticity's sake, so Zara was properly flushed and breathless when they reached her secret room. She glanced quickly up and down the hall, opened the door and pulled him inside.

'OK, you've seen it, now let's go.'

Paul's gaze caressed the forbidden surroundings, his

12

eyes flickering. 'What's the hurry? Now exactly where do you put on your show? Facing the sink or the full-length mirror?'

'The full-length, of course,' she murmured. 'I'll give you a demonstration back at your place. We should get out of here now.'

Instead Paul put his hand to the small of her back and guided her over to face the mirror. He stood behind her. The bulge in his pants pressed lightly against her buttocks.

'So, you stand here like this and then what do you do?'

'Paul, please.' In spite of herself, Zara's knickers grew damp. Her breasts felt heavy and achy, desperate to be touched. Her body was so accustomed to the erotic indulgence that took place before this mirror, it was more than happy to go along with her lover's designs.

'Show me, Zara. Please.'

His voice was sweet and full of need, yet it was the edge of command that made her squirm back against him.

'No one will see you but me.'

Her final protest died in her throat. For after all, wasn't he giving her exactly what she'd dreamed of during those stolen interludes: to be seen and desired by an appreciative male in the flesh?

She began to unbutton her blouse with trembling hands. Paul let out a soft sigh of victory. Her bra unhooked from behind today, but she managed that by pushing down the sagging bra cups so her pink nipples peeped over the top.

She paused. She'd touched herself in his presence before, but only under the blankets, in low light. She'd never been so exposed. The pure exhibitionism of it made her light-headed.

'You're so beautiful, Zara. Please, do it. Do it for me.'

His words melted any lingering resistance. She cradled her breasts and pushed them up as if in offering to him. In the mirror he made a quick motion, as if he wanted to fondle her himself, but then thought better of it.

She took the stiff nipples between her fingers, rolling and tweaking the way she liked best.

'Oh, God, that's so fucking hot,' Paul breathed. Then she saw him shake his head. 'Sorry, sorry. I'll try to stay quiet and just watch.'

'No, please. I like it when they talk.'

'"They?"'

What had she said? But Zara was beyond shame now.

'The men watching. In the mirror. They say rude things to me. But I like it very much.'

Paul's lips lifted in a knowing smile. 'Do you? You like it when a man admits he's got the hardest wood of his life watching you play with your naked tits in the ladies' room when you should be downstairs doing an honest day's work?'

Zara's body jerked. Her knickers flooded with a gush of juices. He'd got it just right.

'Well, do you?' he pressed.

14

'Yes, oh, God, yes.'

'What else do you like to do, you trollop?'

'I … I like to pull down my pants and touch myself while they watch.' Zara stammered out the words, but she found, to her surprise, that the sound of her own voice saying naughty things aroused her as much as him.

'I most definitely would like to see that little show. In fact, I've been imagining this since the day we met. I sat there in that meeting wondering what you'd look like with your shirt open and your pants pulled down. Sweating and squirming and begging for my prick. Is that what you want? Do you want me to fuck you here in your little self-love nest?'

Zara let out a moan of assent.

'But first you should get yourself nice and wet. Take down your pants like a good girl and show me what you do when you're alone. Not with that toy though. I want to see you get your fingers dirty.'

She fumbled with her belt and pushed her jeans and knickers down so her trimmed triangle of pubic hair was revealed. She jammed her hand between her legs and began to strum. He watched until her knees were wobbling and each breath was a groan.

'Well done. I'm very impressed with your work, Zara, but I have to say I'm disappointed to hear you do your naughty business all on your own when every man in this company would be very motivated by this presentation.'

Zara let out a soft 'oh' of shame and desire. He pressed into her from behind and brought his hands around to cup her breasts. Flicking the nipples devilishly, he hissed in her ear, 'Are you ready for my cock now, love? Do those men in the mirror put their cocks inside you, one after the other, as you lie back on the conference table?'

'No,' she admitted, her eyes fixed on his large hands squeezing her breasts with practised skill. 'I promise them they can have me after I come, but then I do something very bad. I leave them trapped in there with their hard cocks still aching in their pants.'

'Aren't you the little cocktease? Well, that's not going to happen today, is it? I know just how to give you what you deserve. I'm going to lie down on that couch and you're going to ride me like a cowgirl. Take off all your clothes now and get a condom out of your purse. Be quick. Every boss likes an employee who takes directions well.'

Zara was all too happy to follow his instructions. Paul pushed his jeans down to his thighs and stretched out on the couch, looking rather lordly. He watched coolly as she sheathed him, but couldn't restrain a moan when she sank down onto his tool.

'Watch yourself,' he whispered. 'Watch yourself get what's coming to you after teasing all of those poor men with your naughty show.'

Zara ground her clit into him, her eyes dutifully fixed

on her own nude body. The sight gave her a secret thrill. She might look more vulnerable than he did, all dressed and proper as he was, but she knew she held the real power within her naked, radiant flesh. She bucked and whimpered as the sensations intensified in her pussy. Her skin shimmered with a thin film of sweat. She could tell Paul was close, too. Could he hold out for her? She clutched him with her secret muscles, willing herself to finish first.

Then, as if he'd pushed himself inside her head as well as her body, he barked out another order. 'Be quick about it now, Zara. You have to be at a meeting in fifteen minutes.'

It was the perfect touch.

She cried out and rammed herself onto him as the orgasm ripped up through her torso. Bucking and sobbing, she milked him until her contractions faded. Then he began to thrust, up and up into her. She tightened her thighs around him, really riding him like a cowgirl at a rodeo. He grunted like an animal as he emptied himself into her. She watched that in the mirror, too.

She had to admit Paul, too, looked especially radiant after a good orgasm.

Afterwards, they lay together on the couch idly admiring their own reflections.

'Now I know why you enchant every man in the room. You're standing up there all smug and satisfied, still wet and swollen in your knickers, while you lecture us on marketing strategy. On some level we know it, and we're transfixed by every word.'

'Perhaps you might suggest my approach as a model the next time you tell some poor CEO how to improve morale,' she teased.

'First I'm going to have to study your methods further. Do promise you'll invite me back here some time. For professional observation, of course.'

Zara flashed them both a secret smile in the mirror.

That was an action item she was sure to follow up on.

Lather. Rinse. Repeat.
Lolita Lopez

It was all that scratching and tugging that got me so hot. I kept my eyes closed as Blake shampooed my hair. Her perfectly manicured nails scratched my scalp, setting the skin alight with tingles as she swirled her fingertips through my foamy hair. The scent of the ultra-expensive vegan shampoo, a heady mix of peppermint and the woodsy musk of cedar, filled my nose and relaxed me. The soft lavender notes of her perfume complemented the shampoo and left me wanting to inhale more deeply.

As she leaned across me to better reach the back of my head, her small breasts brushed against mine. My eyes flicked open, and I was greeted with the enticing view of her cleavage. I recognised the hot pink push-up bra because I had one just like it in my lingerie drawer at home, albeit in a much larger cup size. The front of Blake's V-neck T-shirt gaped as she continued to scrub my hair. The jiggling flesh right before my eyes left me feeling dizzy and hot. I wondered what it would be like to drag my tongue over the swell of her breast. Would she purr with delight? God, I hoped so.

I found my reaction to Blake a bit puzzling. In twenty-nine years, I'd never been this attracted to another woman. Oh, I'd noticed beautiful women and sometimes found my gaze lingering on the athletic types who'd shared my dorm in freshman and sophomore years of college, but I'd never felt like this. She'd stolen my breath away the first moment I'd clapped eyes on her nearly three months earlier. She'd been standing behind the reception desk, just laughing and gossiping away as I'd approached to check in for my usual salon appointment. I'd nearly tripped over my feet. She looked like some kind of spunky little pixie with her white-blonde close-cropped hair and bright smile. As she beamed at me, I'd experienced the strangest frisson of white-hot delight rushing through my belly.

She was different. She affected me so much more than any other person, male or female, ever had. I couldn't stop thinking of her between visits to the salon. She invaded my dreams and tortured me in my naughtiest fantasies. I wanted her so badly but didn't know how to tell her. I was so out of my league on this one. It was one thing to make a move on a man. I'd been doing that for ages and knew how to play that game. But going after Blake? I didn't even know where to start.

'You seem tense today,' Blake murmured as she worked her nimble fingers through the rich lather coating my locks. She smiled down at me, and my heart melted. 'You should book one of Diana's massages. She's fabulous!'

'Maybe,' I said, my gaze fixed on her smiling mouth. I started to have all sorts of deliciously dirty thoughts that were wholly inappropriate for the salon setting.

'Am I doing your eyebrows today?' Her fingers left my hair, and a second later I heard the spurt of water hitting the basin as she prepared to rinse my hair.

'Yes.'

'Just the eyebrows?' She gave me a pointed look. 'I can fit you in if you'd like to take off a little more than that.'

I squirmed when I realised what she was asking. 'I'm not so sure about doing anything down south.'

She smiled sweetly. 'I'm very gentle.'

Oh, I had no doubt. As she rinsed my sudsy hair, I considered my options. I'd been interested in a Brazilian for a while now, but I'd never been able to work up the courage to book one. I mean, having my eyebrows waxed left me teary and blotchy. Having *that* waxed? I'd probably pass out or scream like a baby.

But as Blake's skilful hands worked conditioner into my hair, I started to wonder what it would feel like to have her hands on me. That was an incredibly intimate procedure. I'd be laid bare to her and completely vulnerable. Just the thought of her soft hands manipulating my flesh left me breathless. How could I survive the real thing?

Blake's fingers massaged the back of my neck as she waited for the conditioner to soak in thoroughly. 'So what do you think?'

'I don't know,' I admitted nervously. 'I'm not a huge fan of pain.'

She grinned mischievously as she kneaded my neck. 'I know a really good way to make you forget about the pain.'

My belly wobbled as her insinuation hit home. Electric zings arced across my chest. My nipples drew tight as visions of Blake's fingers and mouth between my thighs danced before my eyes. Was I really considering putting myself through the hell of a Brazilian wax for the chance to share an illicit tryst with her? Yes. Yes, I totally was considering just that.

Swallowing hard, I met her unwavering gaze and nodded. 'All right.'

She smiled triumphantly. 'Great.'

I vibrated with anxiety and excitement as Blake finished my shampoo and conditioning and wound my hair tight in a towel. She grasped my hand and helped me sit up in the squishy vinyl chair. My gaze fell to our interlaced fingers. She sported an electric-blue manicure that looked so playful and flirty compared to my rather staid French tips. We reluctantly parted hands as I stood and put my hand to the damp towel wrapped around my wet hair.

She gestured to my stylist's station. 'After you get your hair done, I'll find you and take you to one of the private rooms in the back.'

'OK.' My wild emotions settled down a bit as I headed over to my stylist's open chair. Candie draped a cape across my front and fastened it at the nape of my neck. As she unwound the towel and wiggled her fingers through my hair, we discussed how much I wanted trimmed and whether or not I wanted a blow dry and straightening. Once that was settled, she got to work and struck up a conversation with me.

I tried to pay attention, but I kept catching glimpses of Blake in the mirror as she dealt with other clients at the busy upscale salon and spa. We exchanged knowing smiles that sent swarms of butterflies racing through my belly. The quick trim and style was the longest thirty minutes of my life. I wanted out of that chair and into one of those private rooms at the back of the salon. Oh, sure, there was going to be pain, but there was also going to be a lot of pleasure.

And I really wanted to get to the pleasure part.

As Candie whipped free the cape, Blake casually joined us. I tried to keep my excitement in check as the three of us chatted about my hair. The taut string of sexual tension between Blake and me kept pulling us closer and closer together until our arms were brushing. Every tiny contact sent shivers down my spine. God, I couldn't wait a moment longer. I needed to touch her.

She seemed to sense my need and gave a little wave of her hand. 'Come on. I'll get us set up in one of the private rooms.'

Relieved, I shot a quick smile at Candie before pivoting on my heel and trailing Blake to the back of the salon. My gaze shifted to the playful cut of her hot-pink ruffled skirt. It made the black salon T-shirt she wore pop. The sexy swing of her hips enthralled me. I tried not to openly ogle her derrière as we passed by the row of occupied chairs and sinks at the shampoo station, but it was so damn hard to drag away my gaze.

I practically vibrated with anticipation as we neared our room. The knowledge that something awfully naughty and totally against the rules was about to happen left me weak in the knees. My pussy actually pulsed as my clit throbbed and that first slick of arousal seeped from my core. My breasts ached. My nipples begged for attention. I was suddenly very glad of the moulded cups of my bra that hid those stiff peaks. At least they allowed me to maintain an outward semblance of modesty.

I slipped by Blake and into the room she indicated. She flipped the 'occupied' sign on the door. My gut clenched as I heard the telltale snick of the door locking behind us. She leaned back against it and stared at me. I clasped my hands together in front of me and chewed my lower lip. She unsettled me. I was used to being the aggressor in my relationships, but I had the distinct feeling Blake wanted that role.

And I liked it. I found the idea of deferring to her rather intoxicating.

'Why don't you go behind the curtain there and change.' She pointed to a screened-off area in the corner of the room. 'There are paper undies in the drawers marked by size, and some sheets. Just wrap one around your waist and come back to the table.'

My gaze moved to the paper-covered table and the counter covered in waxing supplies. My bravery started to diminish as I spotted the cloth strips and wooden sticks. Then I remembered Blake's offer to make the pain go away. That put a little spring in my step as I headed for the curtain. I made quick work of toeing off my pumps and peeling out of my cuffed trousers and simple panties. I felt a bit ridiculous as I emerged from behind the curtain wearing the paper undies with a sheet wrapped around my waist. Not exactly the sexiest of looks.

I slid onto the table and reclined against the padded top. As I rearranged the sheet across my thighs and lower belly, Blake moved into view and smiled down at me. She'd wheeled over a cart holding pots of hot wax, little spreader sticks and various sizes of cloth strips. She picked up a bottle of lavender-coloured liquid and soaked a cotton ball. Wordlessly, she swept the primer over my eyebrows to prepare my skin for the wax.

My fingers curled into fists at my sides as the hot wax smeared across my skin. This part I could handle. It wasn't until her fingers started to smooth the strip of cloth that the dreadful panicky sensation invaded my belly. I tried not to hyperventilate as I anticipated the rip and sting of the first bit of cloth being lifted quickly from my skin.

A soft yelp escaped my lips as the cotton whooshed free of my skin. I'd been waxing and plucking my eyebrows for the better part of twelve years, and I still couldn't get a grip on the pain. Thankfully, Blake worked fast and efficiently as she shaped my eyebrows.

Try as I might, I couldn't enjoy the feel of her hands on me. My excitement deflated as I realised that, although this illicit tryst we'd planned with secret looks and a bit of innuendo sounded like it would be hot, hot, hot, it was probably going to be torture for me.

'Maybe we won't do the Brazilian today,' Blake remarked as she smoothed the cooling gel across my abused eyebrows with a clean cotton ball. Her fingertips caressed my cheek. 'It's not for everyone.'

I glanced up at her and caught her amused smile. 'How can you tell?'

'Well –' she set aside the cotton ball and stroked my upper arms '– you've ripped the paper under your hands to shreds, and your knees are shaking under that sheet.'

'Oh,' I said a bit sheepishly. I consciously stilled my knocking knees and stretched out my curled-up fingers. 'Yeah,' I replied with a heavy, resigned sigh, 'maybe you're right. No Brazilian today.' I frowned apologetically. 'I'm sorry.'

She looked surprised. 'For?'

'Killing the mood,' I explained.

'Oh, I don't know about that,' Blake murmured as she came around and stood next to my hip. 'We still have a good twenty minutes before someone knocks on the door to see if we're finished and ready to clear out of the room for the next client.'

'Really?' A spark of interest flared in my belly. 'Twenty minutes, huh?'

Blake chuckled and lowered her mouth very close to mine. Her soft breath buffeted my lips. 'Twenty minutes.'

I trembled as she teasingly brushed her pouty mouth against mine. My eyelids drifted together as bliss exploded all around me. Blake's gentle kiss awoke the sensual side of me I'd long neglected. Trapped in the never-ending cycle of work, work, work, I'd suppressed the part of me that hungered for a soft, slow touch, a touch exactly like the one Blake now gave me.

Our tongues tangled as she placed a knee on the low table and pushed off the floor. She straddled my sheet-covered hips and rested her palms on either side of my head. I reached up and cupped the back of her neck, holding her in place as we kissed. Lips sliding, tongues stabbing, we clutched at one another as our mouths mated in a wild dance of lust and pleasure.

She left me breathless and shaking when she sat up again and started to flick through the buttons lining the front of my shirt. She urged me to lift my shoulders so she could reach behind me and undo the clasp of my bra. Soon enough, my breasts were bared to her, my bra awkwardly shoved out of the way. She bent low and captured a nipple between her lips. I gasped at the sharp sensation of her mouth tugging on the tender peak. Her tongue soothingly laved the rosy point before she moved on to the other breast.

I threw my head back as she teased me with her lips and teeth and tongue. My God, I'd never known my breasts were so sensitive. She seemed to possess an uncanny knowledge of what I liked and just how I wanted it. My fingers sifted through her hair as she suckled and nipped. I squeezed my thighs together in a desperate attempt to assuage the pulsing, pounding need building down there.

Blake hummed happily as her lips meandered down my front. She peppered light kisses along my belly and around my navel before moving lower down the table. I trembled with anxiety as she unwound the sheet draped across my hips and took hold of the paper panties. I didn't even have to lift my backside to aid in their removal. Blake ripped them free and tossed the remnants aside.

'Open your legs for me,' she ordered huskily. 'Let me see that pretty pink pussy of yours.'

I nearly fainted at the sound of those dirty words spilling from her cherubic mouth. I didn't hesitate, though, and spread my thighs for her. She petted my sex with soft strokes. I kept the area immaculately landscaped and trimmed. It wasn't Brazilian smooth, but it looked natural and feminine.

'Nice,' she murmured before parting the lips of my pussy with her fingers. 'So pink and wet and soft.' Her finger swirled around my opening, gathering the nectar there and spreading it around. When she circled my throbbing clit, I tensed. The sensation was too much, too soon, but Blake didn't stop. She held my gaze as she slowly stimulated my clit with the tip of her finger. It seemed almost like a dare, and I couldn't back down.

Sure enough, the overwhelming sensation faded to something much more pleasant. I rocked my hips, wanting more of the stimulation she provided, but the little witch stopped the movement of her finger. 'Oh, please,' I begged and pumped my hips.

'Patience,' she whispered and started to scoot down my body. When she settled her face between my thighs, I lifted up on my elbows to watch her. I'd never been tasted by another woman and wanted to savour every moment of it. Her skilful tongue swiped the length of my pussy, and I groaned with pleasure. Her tongue slid lower and delved into my cunt, tonguing me in a way I'd never experienced. I panted and clawed at the table as she tongue-fucked me. Her nose nestled between my folds and rubbed against my clit in a way that made my toes curl.

When she'd had enough of tormenting me, Blake traced my labia and turned her full attention to my clit. Her tongue swirled and flicked over the tiny pink nub. I clutched at her head as she devoured me. The rhythmic flutter of her tongue sent little shockwaves through my belly. The fiery prickle of a building climax invaded my core. I pumped my hips, pressing my cunt against her expert mouth, and tried not to cry out or betray us to anyone outside the room.

She didn't make it easy. Blake penetrated me with a pair of fingers and searched for that spot that made me see stars. She slurped my clit between her lips and thrust her fingers at a faster pace. I clapped my hand over my mouth to prevent any sound from escaping. Blake showed no mercy as she lapped at my clit and pumped my pussy with her fingers. She pushed me closer and closer to the edge until, suddenly, I lost control.

Mouth agape and hips rocking, I came hard against her mouth. She never let up, not even a bit. She forced my orgasm to continue, flicking her tongue over my clit as I shuddered and convulsed atop the table. When I couldn't take any more, I reached for her face and touched her cheek in a silent bid for mercy. She chuckled softly as she abandoned my clit. I dropped back to the table with a thud and draped my arm over my face as I tried to catch my breath.

Blake leisurely kissed her way up my body until we were nose to nose again. I cupped her face as I kissed her, my tongue tracing her lips and gathering my musky essence from her skin. She smiled down at me and stroked my cheek. 'You're really beautiful after you come. I mean, you're glowing.'

'Yeah?'

'Mmm-hmm,' she murmured and nipped at my neck.

'And what about you?' I cupped her backside and gave it a playful pat. 'Do you glow after you come?'

That mischievous spark I was beginning to love glinted in her eyes. 'Would you like to find out?'

I nodded but then added, 'I've never done this before.'

She shrugged and gave me a sweet kiss. 'We all start somewhere, right?'

'Sure.'

'Would you like me to show you how?'

'Please.'

She hopped off the table just long enough to peel out of her undies and tuck the ruffles of her skirt into the waistband. We giggled as she jumped back onto the table and our foreheads knocked together. I sensed she was just as excited as I was uncertain.

'Scoot down,' she instructed. 'I need somewhere to put my knees.'

I did as she asked even though I wasn't sure what she planned to do. When she straddled my shoulders, a knee on either side of my head, I finally got it. Her smooth, waxed pussy rested mere inches from my mouth. I caressed her thighs as she manoeuvred into place, and licked my lips with anticipation.

'Do you remember how I licked you?'

'Hell yes,' I replied with a laugh. My body still ached with the reminder of the way she masterfully manipulated me.

'Just do that,' she said softly and spread the lips of her cunt for me. 'Put your tongue right here.' She tapped her clit. 'I'm more sensitive on the left side, and I like up and down licks.' She slid her finger down toward her entrance. 'And here too. I want you to taste me here.'

I vibrated with eagerness as she pressed her pussy to my mouth. I allowed my tongue to slip past my lips and touch her clit. The sensation was alien to me but something I decided I liked very much after that first tentative flick. I held tight to her thighs as my tongue slithered between her dewy folds. Her taste, a unique blend of salt and earthen musk, spilled over my taste buds. It was nothing like I'd imagined and yet everything I wanted.

'Oh, yeah, baby,' she whispered enthusiastically. 'Lick my cunt just like that. Put your tongue inside me.'

Her breath hitched as I did what she asked. The warm, soft passage welcomed my stiff invading tongue. That delicious honey tantalised. I couldn't get enough of her sweet pussy. Her little purrs and tiny whimpers spurred me onward. I grew bolder and more confident with my fluttering tongue and discovered the rhythm that worked for her. I couldn't wait to feel her shatter against my tongue and attacked her clit like a mad woman.

Her fingers wound tight in my hair as she approached her climax. When she finally burst, she pulled hard, setting my scalp on fire with a burn that felt so indescribably good. Her clit pulsed against my tongue. It drove me wild. I knew right then and there that this one tryst with Blake just wasn't going to be enough.

When her orgasm ended, she fell onto her side next to me. It was a tight squeeze on the table but we made it work. We kissed and touched and whispered softly to one another. In the back of my mind, I wondered how much time we had left together. It couldn't be much. I didn't want our moment to end, but reality intruded soon enough when one of Blake's co-workers knocked on the door and asked how much longer we'd be.

'Five minutes,' Blake called out as she touched my face. She claimed my mouth in a possessive and demanding kiss that made my head spin.

We reluctantly parted and slipped off the table. While she slipped on her hastily discarded undies, I fixed my bra and shirt. I headed toward the screen to find the rest of my clothes and get dressed. I could hear Blake cleaning up the table and the waxing supplies she'd used on my eyebrows. When I emerged from behind the curtain, I felt a bit shy. I had no idea what would happen next.

'Are you doing anything tonight?' Blake rubbed the table with a disinfectant wipe before pulling down another length of the protective paper sheet.

'Probably some takeout and reality TV,' I replied honestly. 'You?'

She grinned impishly. 'I guess takeout and reality TV.'

Hope exploded in my chest. 'Yeah?'

'I think we've been dancing around this attraction of ours long enough, don't you?'

'Yes! So completely and totally agree.' I quickly added, 'I would have said something sooner, but I just didn't know how.'

'I figured this was the first for you. I decided to wait and see, but I guess I got a little impatient today. I threw out the Brazilian invite to gauge your reaction.' She made an apologetic face. 'Oh, shit. They're going to charge you for a waxing you didn't receive.'

I shrugged. 'Money well spent.'

She laughed and crossed the short distance between us. Her arms slipped around my waist and hauled me tight against her chest. She threaded her fingers through my hair. Our foreheads touched a moment before our lips met in a lingering kiss.

When we separated, I smiled and gave her a squeeze. 'I'll text you with directions later.'

'Great. I'll bring a bottle of wine.'

'And your overnight bag.'

A broad grin curved her mouth. 'Will do.'

We broke apart and headed toward the door. Out in the salon, we walked side by side to the reception desk where Blake handed over my ticket. As I waited to pay my bill, Blake hung around the desk, pretending to check on her schedule for the rest of the afternoon. After settling my bill, including the phantom Brazilian, I turned toward the door. Leslie, one of the aestheticians, stopped me. 'Wow, Caren! You're glowing. Did you have a facial?'

I couldn't squash the laugh that erupted from my throat. The look on Blake's face was priceless. 'No,' I said brightly. 'The glow must be from all the lovely hands-on service around here.'

'Must be,' Leslie happily agreed before moving on to greet her next client.

Blake and I shared one final, secret smile before I left the salon. I'd expected to feel a little sadness at leaving her behind, but I discovered exactly the opposite. Excitement bubbled in the pit of my tummy. I wasn't sure where our burgeoning relationship was going, but I figured, with the big bang that kicked it off, it had to be somewhere great.

Work It
Heather Towne

I don't work for money, I work for sex. And I don't have to work very hard, if I do say so myself. The money just seems to follow all on its own.

It all started when I turned eighteen. I didn't have the brains or ambition for college, but I was sure I had what it took to succeed in the working world. Specifically, I'm a tall, leggy, busty redhead with violet eyes and porcelain skin, and good taste in fashion.

I didn't really try to flaunt my natural charms at first, it just sort of happened by accident – when I showed up for a job interview with a run in my stocking and buttons missing on my blouse.

I saw the ad in the paper for a secretary at the office of the local diocese. And by the time I'd travelled two bus routes and fought my way through throngs of people and a wicked west wind, I found that I'd lost the two top buttons on my green satin blouse and had picked up a long run in my sheer pantyhose, from my right knee all the way up to my thigh. And there was no time to take corrective action because, by the time I noticed the wardrobe malfunctions, I was already inside the Bishop's office, being interviewed for the job.

He stared at my chest when I stuck out my hand to shake his, then at my legs when I sat down and crossed them. 'Uh, yes, Ms. Songaard, what, uh, experience do you have for this particular job?' Bishop McKenzie asked me. His soft voice kind of broke, and his brown eyes widened, as I reached up and fluffed out my wavy red hair, thrusting my chest out even more.

'Well, um,' I explained, smoothing my hand over the bare flesh exposed on my thigh below my short white silk skirt. 'None really, I guess. I just got out of school, you see. But I'm willing to learn – eager to learn new things.' I batted my long, blackened eyelashes.

Bishop McKenzie was small and sort of delicately featured, with a handsome face and slim figure. He wasn't the stuffy church person I'd expected at all. He looked at my thigh and chest and smiled and said, 'You're enthusiastic?'

'Very!' I smiled back.

He cleared his throat, refocused his eyes. 'Typing skills?'

'I text a lot.'

'Accounting knowledge?'

'I get a bank statement every month.'

'Receptionist duties?'

'Oh, I'm on the phone all the time.'

I pulled my skirt down and sort of folded my blouse together. And Bishop McKenzie almost leapt out of his chair like he wanted to stop me.

'I think I'll take a chance on you, Ms. – Ellen,' he said, smiling warmly. 'I know how difficult it can be for a young person to get started in the labour force these days –'

'Really?'

'– and I think you'll be a quick study.'

I gushed, 'Thank you, Bishop McKenzie!' jumping up and grabbing the man's hand again.

He squeezed my hand with both of his. 'You can call me Derek,' he said, eyes sparkling and teeth shining. 'We're all pretty informal around here. You can start right away?'

'E-mmediately!'

* * *

The work was pretty easy. It was a small office, just me and an older woman who was supposed to train me to take over from her when she retired in a couple of years. She answered the phone, opened the mail, typed up the correspondence and made entries in the accounting system. Most of the time I was with Derek. He always seemed to have some special job for me to do.

Like a day after I'd started, he got me to help him set things up for the Sunday service in the church attached to the office. He gave me a quick tour of the old building, guiding me along by the elbow. I gaped at the big stained-glass windows, the elaborate sculptures and woodwork. 'Do you attend church on a regular basis, Ellen?' he asked.

'No, never,' I replied.

He squeezed my elbow. 'We'll have to change that. It can be quite a moving, rewarding experience, you know.'

'OK.'

He got me to polish the altar – a big old oak table with huge scrolled legs. And when I was bending across it to reach a corner spot, I felt him sort of brush up against me from the back with the crotch of his dark pants. I was wearing a short red skirt, my long legs sheathed in white nylon stockings. I guess I gave him a pretty good view of my bum bent over like that, and he seemed to appreciate it, judging by the bulge in his pants that I felt rubbing against me.

'You're – you're a very … charming young woman, Ellen,' he gulped, like his collar was choking him. He grasped my waist tighter, rubbed his crotch against my bum harder. His bulge pushed my red satin panties right into my butt crack. He looked so handsome and powerful in his black suit with the white collar, the stained-glass window lit up with the sun right behind him.

Maybe I was having a religious experience or whatever they call it, but I got real excited, too. I was wearing a sleeveless white blouse with no bra, and my nipples tightened with feeling, pressing into the silk. My pussy tingled and dampened in my panties. I sort of shifted my bum up and down, helping Derek rub his swelling erection against me. He closed his eyes and tilted his head back, saint-like.

Then he rubbed even harder, really pumping me. And by the way he was gritting his teeth and shaking, it looked like he was already close to coming. I wasn't at all sure there would be a second coming, so I had to get in on the first. I was hot and bothered myself.

I pushed away from the altar table, shoving Derek back. Then I spun around, ripped my blouse open and tore my skirt off, offering up my body to the man of God. It seemed the right thing to do.

Derek grinned ecstatically, taking up my large breasts in his soft, warm hands, staring at them with glazed eyes. He caressed my boobs, his brushing fingers and cupping palms making my cherry-red nipples explode outward with emotion. He captured my buzzing tit-tips between his slim fingers and rolled them. I flung my arms around his neck and excitedly kissed him, swirling my tongue inside his mouth.

For a minister, he really knew his way around a woman's body. He pulled his bright pink tongue out of my mouth and brought it down to my breasts, spun it all around my jutting nipples.

'Oooh, Father!' I moaned, sliding my fingers into his hair and grabbing his head. 'Reverend! I mean, Derek!'

He sucked one of my vibrating nipples into his warm, wet mouth and tugged on it with his plush lips while gripping and groping my boobs. Then he bounced his head over to my other breast at the urging of my fingernails in his scalp, and sucked on that needful nipple. I shivered with delight, chest flaming.

Derek's hands dropped off my tits and down onto my panties. I helped him skin the dampened underwear down my legs, jumping in my red leather high heels to clear them from my feet. My boobs shuddered in his face, and he just had to suck on them some more before he dropped down to his knees at the ginger-furred altar in between my legs, and blessed my pussy with his lips.

'Oh, Father!' I yelped, grabbing his head again and splashing his face into my pussy.

I was so-o-o wet and juicy, super-sensitive. Derek clutched my mounded butt cheeks and dragged his tongue up and down my slit, licking my lower lips, my puffed-up clit.

It felt wonderful! I wetted his tongue even more with

a hot squirt of my juices. He'd been the one about to come prematurely, but now it was me, inspired by the holy man's unholy skill at lapping a girl's snatch.

'Faster, Father! Lick me harder, Father!' I cried.

His fingernails bit into my butt cheeks, his head bobbing wildly in my hands as he lapped me with a wicked intensity, lifting me almost right up out of my heels and into heaven on the end of his tongue. I just couldn't hold back. Not when he slapped at my buzzing button so knowingly.

'Oh, God!' I screamed (and it was never more appropriate). Orgasm exploded inside my pussy and crashed through my quivering body. I came and came, riding the man's face to wicked satisfaction.

I flopped back on the altar table, exhausted and exhilarated. A not-so-virginal sacrifice to the god of lust.

* * *

Bishop McKenzie got reprimanded and transferred to a rural diocese. Because old Mrs. Land, my office mentor, had been watching us from the vestry, and reported what she'd seen to the higher-ups.

I got fired. But not before getting a nice settlement from the church. They were afraid I was going to sue them for sexual harassment or something. They were kind of sensitive about lawsuits, apparently.

* * *

I didn't stay unemployed for long. A big high-profile, high-risk businessman hired me to work at his real estate office. He cared even less about my lack of job skills than Derek had.

Bob Brophy was into appearance, cosmetic and otherwise, with his blow-dried blond pompadour and face-lifted face, his manicured hands and immaculate tan, his fancy suits and ties. He was in his mid-fifties, I guess, and still very good-looking despite, or because of, all the plastic surgery and professional primping. He liked what he saw of me, too, what I added to his glamorous penthouse office on the ninetieth floor of his self-named building.

But he was very demanding.

'Get my wife on the phone, Ellen!' he barked at me my very first day on the job.

I set my nail file down on his gigantic desk, stood up and smoothed down the short, tight black leather skirt he'd bought me to go along with the low-cut blue satin blouse. I leaned over his desk for the phone at his elbow, and he admired the view. I picked up the receiver and punched the button labelled 'WIFE'.

When I handed him the phone, he said, 'I think I lost a cufflink under your chair. Check for me, huh?'

I counted one cufflink on each of his two French

cuffs, but I smiled and turned and bent down anyway, and looked under my chair. I almost split my skirt at the back, and Bob's sharp intake of breath almost sucked me right into his mouth. But then his wife came on the line, and he started talking to her.

I turned back around. He signalled at me to look under his desk. I nodded and crouched down, peered into the opening that split his huge desk in two. That's when I saw that he actually wanted *me* to suck *him* into *my* mouth. His cock was sticking out of his suit pants, pointing at me, pampered and pumped as the man himself.

He kept right on talking to his wife, as I got down onto all fours and crawled under his desk. There was plenty of room, the carpet sort of worn down. I reached up and grasped Bob's penis, stroked it. He didn't miss a beat, just grunting and bucking slightly, babbling to his wife about how much he loved her. I slid my lips over his smooth, swollen hood and engulfed it with my mouth.

'Yeah!' Bob bellowed into the phone. 'Of course I'm faithful to you, honey!'

I placed my hands on the man's spread thighs and sat on my heels, taking more of his power cock into my mouth. He was really built down below, and I think it was all real – tasted like it, anyway. His cock pulsed in my mouth, half of the thick meat locked in between my lips. I slid a hand down his thigh and dug his balls out of his silk shorts, coddled them in my palm.

'Fuck! You're the best, sweetheart!'

His nut sack was smooth as the rest of him, scented like his cologne. I squeezed his balls as I bobbed my head up and down, sucking on his cock. His free hand found my face and slapped my cheek, then grabbed my hair. He moved his hips in his fine leather chair, pumping my mouth in rhythm with me sucking on his pole, still sweet-talking his wife on the phone.

I knew I was doing more than a satisfactory job on his cock and balls, because I tasted salty pre-come bubbling out of his slit. I sucked it up, swallowed it down.

'Jesus, fuck, I love you, baby!'

Bob slammed the phone down. 'That oughta hold the bitch for a day or two!' He pulled his cock out of my mouth, slapped my tongue with it. 'Get up,' he said. 'I wanna show you something.'

When I backed out from under his desk, the building tycoon was standing next to one of the floor-to-ceiling windows that walled his enormous office. He was stroking his spit-slick erection, gazing out at the city below.

'Over here! Come over here.' He pointed with his left hand at a building under construction ten or so blocks away. 'See that?' He gestured with his hand and his dick. 'That's the Brophy Arms. Gonna be an eighty-storey apartment building. Rent starting at two thousand bucks a month. Maybe I can reserve an apartment for you, huh?'

I smiled and took his hard-on into my hand,

appreciatively stroked the sleek tool. But Bob was past that point. He was a busy man. And thoughts of fucking future tenants with astronomical rent made him anxious to fuck little old me.

He shoved me up against the window and pushed my skirt up over my bum. I wasn't wearing any panties, as per his office dress code, and he slotted his cock into my pussy, filling my tingling tunnel with his hot, throbbing meat.

'Oh, Bob!' I groaned, splaying my hands and tits up against the glass, thrusting my butt out at the man behind.

'It's gonna be something special, all right. Steel girder and concrete slab construction, real marble in the –'

He went on and on like he likes to do, always selling. His cock felt terrific sliding back and forth in my pussy, swelling me, surging me full of dizzy heat, to go with the dizzy view. I stared out the window at the sky and the buildings, and it was almost like I was flying, propelled by Bob's churning prick in my cunt.

'Every suite will have its own fireplace, a Jacuzzi, and *two* walk-in closets! The kitchen counters are gonna be granite, with –'

He never stopped, just got more excited. I didn't want him to stop, plenty excited myself. My palms squeaked on the window, big tits rattling the huge pane in rhythm to Bob's banging. Juices started running down my quivering legs, started flowing, started gushing.

'Oh, Bob!' I screamed. 'You've sold me! You've sold me!'

He loved that, stopping his pitch long enough to grunt and jerk, shoot hot come into my leaking pussy. I vibrated out of control, bumped up to a suite on Cloud Nine by the hard-humping tycoon, orgasm breaking through me in blissful waves.

* * *

I was 'de-hired', as Bob put it, two weeks later, when his wife, a former Czechoslovakian princess or something, paid an unexpected visit to the office. She took one look at me in my Bob-bought skin-tight green dress with the plunging neckline and rising hemline, the matching four-inch open-toed heels, and started squawking like a mad hen. Her language was less than regal.

Bob gave me a nice severance package, however, and a promise of future accommodation in that new building of his. But I learned from a horny payroll clerk that I'd just joined a long list of 'personal assistants' who survived in the company only until Mrs. Brophy showed up at the office for an inspection. There were enough laid and laid-off women to fill every floor of that new skyscraper of Bob's.

* * *

Another job popped up right away, wouldn't you know it. I just happened to be strolling down the street window-shopping when a woman suddenly rushed out of a ground-floor office and hired me on the spot. She was the wife of a political candidate running for governor of the state. Her name was Greta Torsten, his Turner Torsten, and she said I'd be just perfect for the job she had in mind.

Greta was a kind of severe-looking woman with short grey hair, hard grey eyes and a whip-thin flat body. Her husband was silver-haired and red-lipped, with pale-blue eyes and a strong chin, quite handsome for an older man, judging from the posters of him plastered all over the office. 'He's sure to win,' Greta assured me. 'He's a former alderman, mayor and state senator, has all the skills and contacts necessary for the job.'

'Oh, I know!' I responded, even though I'd never heard of the guy before. I hadn't even voted in an election yet. But I've found it pays to be nice and agreeable on the job.

'Yes, well, I want you to meet my husband, get to know him. Tonight. In Dominion City. He's giving a speech to a swine association up there. And I want you to see him after he's done campaigning.'

'You bet!'

'Do you –' she turned to look at one of the giant posters of her husband '– think Turner will be "attractive" to the voters?'

48

'Oh, yes!' I gushed, drawing a wince from the great man's wife.

She supplied me with a car and the name of the hotel and the room number where her husband was staying. Told me to knock on his door around midnight, say I had a campaign contribution for him (a joke, I guess). I was to wear the same short pink ruffled skirt and white tube-top and knee-high white boots I was already wearing.

She was the boss.

So I drove out to Dominion City and knocked on Room 1055 of the Mercantile Hotel at midnight, and Turner himself opened the door, looking even more handsome in person. He was wearing just a white bathrobe, his silver hair slicked back, face and hands and legs tanned a deep brown. He held a drink in his hand, and I could smell more on his breath.

'Room service!' I yelped, mixing things up a bit. Sometimes you have to use your own initiative on a job. Employers usually like that.

Turner loved it. He grinned brilliant white teeth and pulled me inside the room. He crowded up close to me, touching my hair, stroking the wavy red tresses. 'You're one of my supporters?' he sort of slurred.

'Any way I can!'

My enthusiasm rubbed off on him. His cock rose up and peeked out from between the flaps of his bathrobe.

The impressive organ was as polished as the rest of him, full of pep for such an old man.

Turner set his drink down and shouldered his robe off, fully exposing himself. He was one fine politician. 'Will you sit on my face?'

I was a little surprised at that. But more than willing to have a seat, built as I am with the necessary equipment for that sort of job.

Turner stretched out flat on his back on the bed, his cock jutting out over his stomach, and he watched as I stripped off my skimpy duds. Then I climbed onto the bed with him, over his face. He grabbed onto my butt cheeks and pulled my bum down closer.

'Yikes!' I squealed, when I felt his hot wet tongue squirm into my butthole.

I reached backwards and grabbed onto the headboard of the bed for support, Turner peeling my buttocks apart and spearing his tongue deep into my chute, writhing it around inside my anus. I'd never had anyone tongue my ass before, least of all an expert. Turner had a silver tongue, all right. It felt all weird and wicked, the guy plugging into my bum and shooting me full of electricity.

After digging around inside my rear tunnel for a long, tingling while, he slowly slid his mouth-organ out of my chute. And then he started licking my bum crack, painting my sensitive butt cleavage with the broad, damp, budded brush of his tongue.

I jerked, boobs jumping and bent legs quivering. Turner was even better at licking ass than Reverend McKenzie had been at licking pussy. He stroked my crack, teased my rosebud, setting my bum and body ablaze.

'Sit right down on my face!' I heard him rasp from below. 'Please!'

Polite, as well as dirty. No wonder the ass-kisser was such a popular politician. I splatted my bum down on his face.

How he could breathe, I don't know, because my cheeks splayed right over his face, covering up his nose and mouth. But he revelled in. I could feel him washing his face in my heated rump, plying my taut butt flesh with his fingers, sucking in deep of my ass.

Until he gently pushed me off and gasped, 'I want you to fuck me now. Fuck me in the ass.'

Was he a closet homosexual? I don't know. His wife *was* rather mannish.

But I quickly found out that he was at least a suit-case pervert, because that's where he kept his strap-on. I should say *my* strap-on, because I was the one who ended up wearing it.

Turner helped me fasten the black leather straps to my hips and butt, and adjust the foot-long black dildo that jutted out from the leather platform covering my pussy. Then he sprawled back out on the bed, closer to the edge this time. He lifted his legs up and held them, presenting his cute little butt to me.

I oiled the big dong with the lube he provided, then squirted some onto his butthole. He spasmed, his cock jumping. His ball sack was hairy, tightened with feeling, his rear opening not quite as hairy, but even tighter.

I gripped my borrowed cock and looked down at the laid-out public figure. 'Are you sure –'

'Fuck my ass!'

I plunged into his hole. I'd had no experience at this sort of thing, but like at all my other jobs, I just dove right in, bulbous plastic head first. And kept on going, poling almost the entire twelve inches of strapped-on dildo into Turner's ass. He received the results with a groan of pure delight.

I wrapped my hands around his thighs and pumped my hips, fucking like I'd been fucked so many times. The dildo glided back and forth in his chute. He moaned and ran his hands all over his silver chest, latching his fingers onto his prominent pink nipples and rolling them like a woman would, rolling his head around on the bed.

It looked super-erotic, the man's big cock jumping every time I thumped my thighs against his butt, drove dong up his ass, his body spread out wantonly before me. And it felt super-erotic, the leather dildo mount pressing into my ginger pussy with each pump, until it was glued to my wet, buzzing loins.

'Fuck me harder! Faster!'

I went up to ramming speed, slamming in and out of Turner's stretched, gaping bumhole. I shouldered his legs and grabbed onto one of my tits, squeezed the shimmering mass, pulled on the electrified tip. I grasped his cock with my other hand, pumping the rock-hard tool and his sucking ass at the same time.

His cock pulsated in my shifting hand. Then it surged, sprayed. 'Pay-off!' he hollered, his entire body jerking, come blasting out of the tip of his spasming dick and striping his heaving chest and stomach.

My hips flew, pussy smouldering to the ignition point. I drilled happiness into Turner's butt, jetted joy out of his cock. And then I shuddered with my own fiery ecstasy, the wet-hot friction on my pussy setting me ablaze with orgasm.

Just as Greta stormed into the room and snapped a picture.

'You won't divorce me now, you bastard!' she yelled. 'Not with this incriminating evidence hanging over your head. I'm damned well going to be First Lady one of these days!'

We both stared at her, the pair of us still shivering with orgasmic aftershocks, my cock still buried up Turner's bum, his cock still seeping sperm in my clutching hand.

* * *

I took a nice monetary vow of secrecy and quit the team. Greta wanted me to work at her late daddy's bottling plant as an executive assistant. But I turned her down. It didn't look like something, and she didn't look like someone, I'd enjoy doing. And shouldn't you love what you do, and how you do it, and who you do it with?

That way, it's hardly work at all.

Peaches
Lizzie Behan

I think I formed my crush within thirty seconds of seeing her. I don't think I have ever witnessed anyone prettier, although perhaps infatuation makes me biased. I'm sure plenty of people would disagree with me, but that is their loss.

The first thing I saw was her big bottom. The material of her black skirt was stretched to near-breaking point as she bent to tidy some paperwork into a low drawer. There were no lines interrupting the smoothness of her curve. The fabric clung tight, hemming in the wide hips and plump thighs, squeezing in the flesh down to her knees where the netted stockings became visible, confining her large but firm calves, their definition aided by the high heels she wore. In my mind the vision came of her skirt splitting down the middle with the stress at its seam, the material shrinking away as her soft white globes of bum flesh were exposed, the whole beautiful rump thrust tantalisingly out towards me. I have to admit, I felt a rush of excitement seep from my pussy to soak into my knickers. She straightened up, turned around and saw me flushed and open-mouthed before her. And then she smiled and lit up my world, and I fell instantly in love.

Her name is Samantha but my pet name for her is Peaches. It isn't something I say to her face of course. It's just a name in my head, to add to my thoughts when I dream of lying next to her, snuggling into her warmth. That first night I dreamt of her, all I pictured was her lovely face, that first smile she gave me. That image alone was enough to make me come. If you saw her you would know why. You don't actually notice the extra weight around her neck unless she tucks her chin right in, and even then I love it. Some might say it defines her as fat but to me it just shows her opulent softness, the joy you would feel in putting your arms around her and holding her to you.

Beneath her foundation her skin is white-pink and young. She has large blue eyes and always wears black mascara to accentuate her long lashes. She mostly wears her shoulder-length hair tied back, leaving an expanse of smooth forehead down to her neatly arched dark eyebrows – an oddity when her hair is naturally blonde. Stranger still, you never really notice this darkness unless her hair and fringe is down. This gives her an even younger look, like she is still the schoolchild of her Facebook photos, not the woman in her late twenties of today. Her mouth is small but with slightly plump, very kissable lips, the top one curled ever so slightly upwards, like a miniature ski jump. And when she smiles the sun comes out, and no one but no one could fail to lose their heart.

It's not only the brightness in her eyes but the sheer width of the smile, not just in the mouth but in her soft pale cheeks. They form little morsels of smooth, firm flesh. And 'firm' is the key word here because it is what some doubters fail to see. Some women *are* fat, with saggy rolls flowing over bulging bellies, whereas others, like my Samantha, are simply carrying extra weight. Sometimes it's a lot of extra weight, particularly around their hips, but there is no sag, no flabby flesh. There's maybe a little belly paunch but that is *always* sexy, and there is no cellulite either. The flesh is dense, pulling the skin smooth and tight over it, so that it glistens like a plump juicy sausage in a pan. The fingers and toes may be podgy but the breasts and bum and limbs will still be shapely and *firm*. When they get older, the tautness may begin to go and gravity will take its toll, but while still young these beauties will just be the pale-skinned epitome of blissful comfort, delicious beings to immerse oneself in and cuddle and love. The sight and feel of them naked is surely the most precious and alluring experience.

It is hard to describe her character without sounding sycophantic. She is bright, funny, bubbly, clever. Everything about her makes me realise how flawed my own character is. She is friendly and attentive, flirty, suggestive and completely addictive. She seems so assured and can certainly set hearts and cocks pounding, although under her façade of confidence she is perhaps a little insecure, no doubt because of her weight and the stigma blinkered society places on all but the stick-thin. All the boys love her and want to bury their undeserving pricks into her from behind, to ride her scrumptious bum, to squash and slap against those cushion cheeks and spurt inside her with no intention of ever giving her the time of day afterwards. She is infinitely fuckable but I see way beyond that, despite the number of hours I dream about her body next to mine, our tongues and fingers inside each other, our wet pussies kissing. I see her as my angel and I idolise her because she is perfection, a beauty that great artists would paint and immortalise. I wish I could be more of a match for her but I am not. I am quite pretty and petite but my shyness is crippling and I have nothing of her charms, nothing to make her choose me over the countless others who must love her too.

I got a job at the department store straight from school and met her on my first day there. I was nervous and disorientated but she took me under her wing even though I was on handbags and she was the assistant manager on lingerie. She made it her business to support me, out of the kindness of her heart. I just stared and smiled at her and tried to control the flutters inside. I have been there a year now and I want her more each day. I am a natural introvert but I slowly managed to get closer to her, mainly due to her open nature and because when I shake off my inhibitions I can be quite funny. Every time we talk and laugh together it takes me hours to come back down. She is so exhilarating but I cannot find a way to tell her. I don't have the confidence to lay my heart on the line, especially since I consider myself so much her inferior. I am a simple soul destined to be passed by. All I really want is to be hers and adore her forever and to let her know how beautiful she really is.

I have stored up every little detail I could about her and cherished them. Each scrap that tells of her private nature is more valuable to me than diamonds. I furtively watch her, heart pounding, while she sorts and manhandles the lingerie for display. I try to gauge which her favourite items are, which she would like to own, just so I can picture her in them.

She always wore stockings and high heels, always under tight above-knee skirts that showed off the girth of her legs and the curve of her big sticky-out bottom. Her bum was so big it constantly fascinated me. Every time I saw it my belly flipped and my pulse was sent racing. If you looked from the back it was just a little wider than most, but from the side it had a pussy-wetting jut, coming out from her back almost like a Victorian bustle, then flattening slightly under the pressure of her skirt before curving in at the full, rounded tuck. Oh, to have it naked in your face – all warm and bare, all smothering softness, the crack so deep and pungent ...

I am a secret pervert it seems, although I never fully knew it until I saw Samantha. It was she who made me crave the pillow cheeks of a plump girl's bottom, the lovely soft belly under your own, the big silken thighs open around you. And it was she who made me realise the unutterable delight of a thick-legged girl in stockings. To me, the most captivating sight would be that of a beautiful girl with a big round bum, naked from the waist down except for her fishnets and high heels. That's how I always picture her, almost every night and even during the day sometimes if it is all too much for me.

Before I dream up yet another scenario with the two of us together, kissing and cuddling and fucking, I always see her in my mind's eye, her back to me, wearing her shiny black heels and whichever pair of stockings I secretly saw her holding that day, bent slightly forward, her sweet podgy hands reaching behind and her nails painted either black or red, gently digging into the flesh of her gorgeous, massive, sexy bum, with its long, deep crack only very slightly parted to make me dream of what lies inside.

You can see why I usually keep all this to myself, can't

you? I'm meant to be a normal, wouldn't-say-boo-to-a-goose type of girl, but every night my head rages with such rude thoughts, of secretly spying on big girls' bums and then making love to them. In mitigation, in case you think I'm just some chubby-chasing slut, let me tell you that I've yet to make love to any such woman and the ingredients required have to be precise for me to be turned on. Crucially, the girl has to be *very* pretty. If this is the case her bum can be as big as it wants and I will always lust after it. If the girl isn't pretty, the bum does absolutely nothing for me. Similarly, a pretty girl without a nice big arse leaves me cold with disappointment, especially a big girl, one of those with a wide flat backside and no jut at all. Like I say, the prettier the girl, the rounder the rump can be, and the combination is vital. This is actually very rare, which is why Samantha is so special.

And that is why it almost tore my heart out to discover that she was dating an old schoolfriend. I had never really believed she could fall for me as hard as I had for her but I lived in hope that the way she smiled at me actually meant something more than mere friendship. It was crushing to have confirmation that she did indeed go for guys after all, and therefore I couldn't feature in her most secret thoughts, despite what my instincts told me. Ironically, I think my infatuation only deepened once I learned all this, just to prove what a pathetic specimen I really am.

I guess my stocking fetish truly kicked in at this point too. I think it was an attempt to shift my focus away from her and leave her be, but she nearly always managed to creep back into my fantasies at some point. I have become obsessed with hosiery, specifically when it is shown off to its absolute best: when it is worn by a young, thick-legged girl. Every dream I have involves stockings or tights. Every time I masturbate I take some to bed with me. Sometimes I can come just from the feel of the nylon on my inner thighs or lightly brushing over my puss. Other times I gently rub myself while smoothing them over my tits and belly. Sometimes I would put my hand inside one stocking to play with myself, or put a pair of tights on and rub my pussy through the sheer fabric. It embarrasses me to say that when I have come, I often push the dampened gusset into my mouth and begin rubbing myself again. Really, if you had ever met me you wouldn't believe I'm capable of such perversions. I am just so Little Miss Average, so normal and straight-laced, I simply don't know where it all comes from. I have to blame Samantha, since I never had the slightest interest in stockings until I saw her in them.

I bought my first vibrator with my second pay-packet, along with a harness to strap it on – the latter being an aid to add spice to my fantasies rather than something I ever dreamed I would get to use for real. I had to hide these items carefully and they only came out when I was sure my parents would not be back to disturb me. The toys only made me worse and took my naughtiness to a higher level. My orgasms became more intense with the vibrator and so my imagination had to step up the rudeness in order to keep pace. Wearing the harness brought out a side of me I didn't know existed. It had a little vibrating pad inside that could bring me off as I wore it. I loved to oil it up and stroke it slowly like it was my own real cock, kneeling on my bed, watching myself in the mirrored door of my wardrobe. I sometimes got two pillows side by side and folded them over in a terribly crude and frankly disrespectful representation of my darling Samantha's bottom. I would hold the pillows in their folded state and push the strapped-on dildo between them and jerk my hips back and forth, dreaming that I was thrusting my angel from behind. I even used to leave the pillows by an open window first, to give them that cold softness I knew she would have.

I am embarrassed to admit that another time I struggled home with two watermelons and put them together to act as her imaginary bottom, shoving the dildo between them and pumping hard, just to try and create the sound my groin and thighs would make slapping against her backside. I felt almost schizophrenic doing this, like some mad woman was inside me, but I know the darker thoughts were just caused by frustration at not having her. If it came to reality I would return to my mouse-like submission, loving her as tenderly as I could. Sometimes I wore a netted stocking over my head when I fucked the pillows, or stuffed one leg of a pair of tights in my mouth and the other one up my puss. One time I pushed a very sheer nylon stocking up my bottom and slowly withdrew it as I came, thinking of her naked arse of course.

Out of the blue a chance materialised. There was a charity event in the store and Samantha was trading kisses for a pound donation. For hours I watched her laughing away as the old-timers and the teenage jack-the-lads popped in their coins and tried to hit her lips when all she was offering was a cheek. I kept running over my game-plan in my head but my legs were shaking and my belly turning somersaults and I remained rooted to the spot. Some of those chancers would put their arms around her – more contact with her than I had ever had. Every day I dreamt of melting into her comforting body. I would have given anything to be in her embrace and feel the gentle softness enveloping me, and these guys were putting their hands all over her for a quid!

I only summoned up the courage after lunch. I waited for a quiet moment when she was alone, walked up to her, showed her the ten-pound note in my hand and quickly stuffed it into the collection box. I couldn't afford such extravagance but what the hell! Not surprisingly she looked a little taken aback.

'You must think it's a good cause!' she said with a shy laugh.

'What do I get for that?' I said, trying to muster an air of nonchalance. 'I reckon I deserve a proper kiss for that amount!'

She laughed but looked a little confused and I could already feel my courage draining away and my words sounding crass and stupid. I hastily backtracked, talking over her before she had a chance to speak and turn me down.

'Only joking!' I laughed. 'Yeah, it really is a good cause – I always give generously! If I don't get any better offers I'll be back for my kiss later!'

I was grinning but dying inside and my face was red with the stress and humiliation. She managed a nervous smile as I beat my hasty retreat. The thing was, despite my defeat I couldn't let this opportunity go. It was my best chance ever of gaining some close contact. I had to drag myself back up during the afternoon but I was determined not to waste the opportunity. At the end of the day I watched her sign off her till and go into her little stockroom behind the counter. Other staff were milling about so I waited before sneaking over to the door. I still didn't know what to say but by rights she owed me ten kisses and I wanted them. I pushed the door open and to the astonishment of us both I caught her right in the act. She was facing me, her skirt up round her waist displaying her pale thick thighs. Her hands were at her hips, pulling up the string sides of a tiny thong. I could just about see a little black triangle of lacy material between her thighs. She was simply too stunned to pull her skirt back down.

'What are you doing in here?' she said, her voice high and strained.

I'm not sure what reply I mumbled – probably something about wanting my kisses, but I was far too engrossed in staring at her crotch.

'It's not what you think!' she said, sounding panicky now. 'It's just shrinkage!'

I managed to drag my eyes off her and she was finally able to cover her modesty. 'Shrinkage', it transpired, was basically another word for theft. When items were returned faulty they had to be sent to the supplier for a debit. However, most suppliers didn't want them because they knew the items had often been worn for a night out and returned on spurious grounds. She was therefore at liberty to write them off and throw them away. However, since all they often needed was a good wash, it seemed such a waste.

'If I know there is a pair that will fit me,' she said, 'I come to work with no knickers on and then put them on at the end of the day and take them home. I can't put them in my bag because even though they are for the bin, it is still technically stealing.'

I wanted to tell her how many times I had pictured her in just such a pair of panties, so tiny and sexy and tight on her beautiful big body. Anything like this would just sound dirty, like I viewed her only as a sex object in the same way the boys did, when in fact I saw her as the most perfect person in the world. I wanted to tell her she was everything to me and that I could barely cope away from her company for a single minute, that I thought of her all day and wanted to be with her forever. All of this would sound ridiculous, though, so in the end I just said, 'Do you think I should tell someone?'

She stared mute and horrified at me for several seconds.

'No, please don't,' she finally managed to reply. 'If you tell someone I will get fired!'

'Do you not think, then,' I said, 'that you should kiss me?'

She didn't know what I meant so I told her. The best way to keep my mouth shut was to put her lips to it. I had paid for ten kisses and so it was only right. She was still dumbfounded but I was already bearing down on her and she knew she had no choice.

'Maybe a proper one will count for all,' I said with a smile.

Then I put my arms around her, leant in and kissed her. She was too shocked to respond but it was still fabulous. The warmth, her comforting size as I cuddled and squeezed, the softness of her lips and her breasts against me. I kissed her as tenderly as I could, every now and then snaking the tip of my tongue over her closed lips, just delicately, hoping she would open up but not trying to force it. It was all I could do to restrain myself from pulling up her skirt and exposing those gorgeous legs in those netted stockings. I wanted to clutch her arse and grind my crotch into her leg but that would have been gratuitous when she deserved only gentleness. In my dreams, once we kissed she let me sink into her and we were together. In reality she didn't try to fight me but her arms stayed at her sides and didn't gather me in. Her breaths were faltering, though, and I could detect her pounding heart against my own. Just before I broke off I was sure I felt her lips open and her tongue brush mine. She opened her eyes and sucked in her bottom lip to dry the wetness from it. I think she was shaking.

'You are the most beautiful person in the world,' I said.

'You know I have a boyfriend,' she finally whispered.

It wasn't really what I wanted to hear. She was trying to give me the brush-off and it was sending my head spinning. After my declaration she was giving me nowhere to go and I felt cornered and lost, unable to see any way to regain the initiative. In a panic I said: 'Does he know you've been stealing knickers?'

'You aren't going to tell anyone, are you?'

'Not if you let me see them,' I said. 'Bring them to my house to show me and I promise not to tell.'

I didn't want it to sound like blackmail but I guess that's all it was. She looked edgy and afraid, but she still nodded her assent. What else could she do? I told her to come the following night and not to be late. I wanted her to know that I would never hurt her really, so before I left I took her hand and kissed it and told her that I loved her.

She wasn't late. She barely managed a half-smile on my doorstep and hadn't lost any of her nerves from the previous night. I wanted to calm her but I was too excited about the contents of her bag, of digging into it and bringing out handfuls of knickers and suspender belts and tights. I actually wanted to pull down my own underwear and rub my itching cunt all over a big pile of her ill-gotten goods, but I didn't dare tell her that. It was the first time I had ever seen her in jeans and a jumper. She looked sweet but not as ragingly sexy as she did in her work clothes.

'I want to see you in them,' I said.

She started to bite her lip and look anxious but I quickly reminded her of what I could do if she didn't oblige me. I felt guilty as hell but I needed her too urgently to worry about morals. She would see it was for the best. I told her to take the bag up to my room and change, and to wait for me on the bed. I held off for ten minutes before deciding I could wait no more. I almost fainted when I saw her. She was on her side on the bed, her face partially hidden in her arm although I could still see the flush on her cheek. The rest of her body where it was uncovered was milky white and perfectly smooth. To my joy she had chosen a purple basque which pushed her ample tits up and threatened to spill them out. Her fishnet stockings were the same colour and were tight at the top, causing an indentation around the middle of her large thighs. It was such things, those little displays of how soft and abundant her flesh was, that made my pussy drip. I had to go close to the bed and stoop to see any sign of the tiny knickers hidden between her thighs and below her belly. I climbed onto the bed, homing in on her crotch to breathe her in. Her scent was wonderful, sweet and musky.

Suddenly I felt like I was the woman and she the teenager. She seemed so nervous and at my disposal I couldn't believe I had wasted all this time in getting her here. I wanted to taste every inch of her and suck her soft flesh into my mouth. I was trying to kiss her thighs and strip off my clothes at the same time. I could hear her sporadic breaths and see her peeping out from her arm to gauge what was coming her way next. When I was naked I roughly pulled at her arm to force her onto her back. I grabbed at the basque and found she had left it undone in readiness for me. It came away in my hand and I sank onto her, kissing her and pushing my tongue out to find hers.

This time she did respond. Her arms came around me and I was enveloped in her warmth. She gave a huge sigh and I knew she was mine. I ground my bare crotch against her and she writhed beneath me, pulling me in and squashing me to her yielding body. I burrowed down to find her nipples, pleased to see they were cute pink circles with little rigid teats, much smaller than I had envisaged. I drew them in hard and even nipped at them to make her squeal, and then rubbed my little tits into her face and made her return the favour.

I wanted to spend hours kissing and teasing her but was too impatient to get between her thighs, the true hub of her fatness. I tarried a little on her chubby belly with its deep button, but was soon drawn down to lap the insides of her silken thighs and press my face to the lace of her knickers. I could make out the soft bulge of her mound and tell it was shaved bare. I think this might actually have been the most exciting part – it was certainly the most unexpected. I had not realised how delectable the mons would be on a plump girl. It was simply the most kissable pad of squashy flesh you could ever imagine. It was cuppable and spankable like a tiny buttock, the top of the slit a deep crevice between the fat outer lips. I began easing her knickers down but once I began to expose her peachy quim I forgot sensuality and ripped them off.

She smelt full and heady. Her inner lips were actually thin and barely protruded at all, not at all the vulgar petals of my fantasies. She tasted much more subtle than her scent suggested and her slit was delicate, but still the plumpness of all the surrounding tissues made it impossible not to press your face right in and try to suffocate in her. She wriggled and sighed and panted as I pushed into her and plunged my tongue as far up her as I could. I reached up to grasp her juddering tits, pinching and stretching the nipples to make her wail. Then I was burrowing even further down, forcing her legs up off the bed and sucking harshly on mouthfuls of bum cheek, drawing in as much as I could and biting upon it.

My fingers strayed up her cunt and found a pond of warm silky juice inside her. She felt pliant, like you could stretch her infinitely, maybe bathe your whole hand in her cream. I couldn't stop trying to eat her bum and now that I had wrestled her g-string totally off I was turning her, first nipping at her hips and then sinking my teeth into her lovely fat cheeks. I sucked away, covering her in love bites as I forced my fingers in and out of her wet quim. She sounded so young and vulnerable, not at all the bold girl she tried to portray herself as in public. I got her on her front and smacked her rump hard, wobbling her meat and pinking the surface. She wailed but still thrust her hips up, maybe for more or maybe to aid the movement of my fingers still inside her, to let the pleasure they brought counter the pain fizzling across her arse. I used my wanking fingers to haul her onto her knees and then there it was, my holy grail: her magnificent bent-over bum in all its glory.

I had to feast upon it. I had to feel its sheer size and softness against my face, to force my way into that deliciously dank cleft. She rode my fingers as I did the dirty deed. Her sighs were tremulous, although she fought her trepidation and pushed her bottom back to open it against me and let me give her that most scintillating of thrills. She tasted sweeter than I dared imagine. I wanted to pull her right onto me and be suffocated by that beautiful fat bum. I wanted to draw my last breath of air from the deep valley of her arse as she crushed it into me. But more than anything I wanted to fuck her.

I made her stay on all fours and masturbate while I tightened the harness around my waist. It wasn't easy for her to do this rude act in front of me, especially as she was completely visible in the wardrobe door mirror and I could watch her flushed face as she rubbed herself. I let her see me in return, oiling the dildo and stroking it like my own cock. I held her hips firmly and slid the thick toy all the way into her, watching her beautiful face intently, seeing my own break into a smile of triumph as I filled her completely and my groin pressed against her cool flesh at long last.

I should have been gentler but the desire to slap hard against her bum proved instantly irresistible. I could see her arse moving below me and in reflection too, the shock waves rippling through it with each heavy thrust. For me it was an unparalleled thrill to watch her face and bottom at the same time, both at their most wonderful. I could see her bliss in the way she clawed at the bed sheets. I could smell her love for me filling the room. The buzz at my own clit drove me on relentlessly, pushing her mercilessly towards her release.

As her orgasm neared she did the most erotic thing I could possibly imagine: with her eyes still tightly closed she put her thumb into her mouth and sucked upon it like a baby. It wasn't for effect. It was a totally spontaneous, instinctive measure to help cope with the surge of ecstasy about to burst through her – and I thought it was *me* that needed all the comfort!

She now waits for me every day at work and I think it is fair to say that she is besotted. She sneaks moments with me whenever she can, happy for any swift secret contact she can steal. And she steals for me too. I select the stockings or knickers that I want and make her take them for me. They could not possibly fit her so she has to conceal them up inside. She comes to me shaking with the illicit thrill of her actions and I hold her and then kiss her, pulling up her skirt, parting her fat thighs and slowly tugging the hidden stockings or g-string from her pussy. Then I put the item on and wear it while we make love. She wants to be with me all the time, desperate for any chance to envelop me.

The trouble is a new girl has started, a little older than Samantha but still pretty, with a haughty confidence and brilliant white smile against her smooth chocolate skin. And her bum is even bigger, an impossibly round apple-jut that only black girls can have and still retain any shape and softness. My heart races and my pussy melts every time I catch a glimpse of her in those skin-tight skirts and brightly coloured stockings. She is the most captivating thing I have ever seen. But how could a wallflower like me possibly even catch her eye, let alone win her heart? What chance has someone like me got of ever seeing that woman in just her fishnets, bent slightly forward with her red nails digging into those sumptuous cheeks to part them for me? It has to happen, though. Somehow I have to make it happen because I know I simply cannot live without that fat, beautiful black arse.

Military Police
Georgie Taylor

'Pull over,' the MP yelled through his window as he drove his jeep alongside mine.

Fuck! I hadn't seen him coming. I was busy concentrating on the road. It was dark and I was looking for a driveway along the dusty road. We were stationed in Tasmania, Australia, out on the West Coast, a two-hour drive from Hobart. But now we were out in the sticks. Where on earth had he come from? What was he doing here?

I stayed seated, the motor idling as he pulled in behind me. A dozen thoughts flashed through my mind. How was I going to explain my attire, how I'd managed to leave the base and be driving this jeep?

Glancing into my side mirror I could make out that he was tall, the light from his headlights illuminating his physique. Not bad: well built with strong legs. Wondered if I could charm him like I did some of my fellow officers.

He leaned into my window. .

'Have you been drinking?' he asked.

My senses were assaulted by his good looks, piercing eyes and deep sexy voice. 'What? No.' Why on earth would he think that? I'd been driving slowly and carefully.

'Are you sure?' he persisted.

'Yes.'

'Not a drop? It's against army policy – you know that, don't you?' His eyebrow arched inquisitively.

'I assure you I haven't,' I said, slightly annoyed at being delayed for what I was hoping would be a night to remember.

The guy was fucking gorgeous. It was hard for me to concentrate on anything other than his sexy mouth. What sort of a MP was he?

'You were swerving all over the road.'

I was not! But I wasn't going to argue with him.

'Oh, I'm sorry,' I said. 'I'm looking for an address.'

'An address for what? What are you looking for out here?'

'I ... er ...' How was I going to explain I was meeting the rest of the soldiers out here? We'd all be in trouble then.

'Step out of the jeep, please.'

'What for?'

'Just do as I ask.'

Annoyed, I watched him eye me as he opened my door. Being a bit of an exhibitionist, I deliberately left my legs open a fraction longer than necessary. Gave him something to look at – but closed them quickly when I remembered I wasn't wearing my sexiest panties.

'Not quite army attire, now, is it?' he said, indicating my lack of uniform.

'Well ... I ...' Again he had caught me off-guard.

'Your platoon has only just arrived, hasn't it? Yesterday, I believe.'

'That's right,' I said indignantly. I was an officer and not used to being interrogated for something as minor as my driving abilities, in fact I've never had an infringement in my life.

'Licence?'

'You could have asked me before I got out,' I said, becoming more annoyed at his arrogance.

I leaned into the passenger seat. I knew he'd probably be able to see up my skirt so I rummaged around longer than usual.

'Here you go,' I said, batting my eyelashes at him.

He looked from me to the licence.

'This has expired.'

'It has not,' I said, trying to snatch it from him.

He turned me around and slammed me against my car. I tottered on my high heels, trying to regain my balance.

'Hey,' I said, shocked.

'Keep still,' he said, 'or I'll have to arrest you.'

'For what?'

'Being out of uniform for one, and then there's all that make up – isn't there a policy on how much you're allowed to wear?'

'No, there isn't, and if you're going to make an issue out of it I might have to take you up on sexual harassment.'

'Take it easy,' he said. 'This is just routine. I need to frisk you. Spread your legs for me.'

'What?'

'Just do it!'

I liked my men being a bit rough and if he wanted to frisk me I didn't really mind. In fact it had been one of my fantasies for years, getting picked up by a good-looking MP. Thought I should act a bit outraged, though.

'I beg your pardon,' I said, trying to move away from him.

'Hands up on the bonnet, now,' he ordered.

I did as he asked and actually enjoyed the way he ran his hands down my arms, over the insides of my breasts, down to my waist, where they lingered on my hips. Then his hands were running down the outside of my thighs, over my calves and back up the insides, where they hesitated at that soft fleshy part for a moment before cupping my pussy.

I gasped. 'What do you think you're doing?'

'You have a problem with that?' He squeezed.

79

What on earth was I supposed to say? How do you react when someone in authority takes advantage of you?

'No,' I said, deciding to play along with him.

'What about this?'

His fingers grabbed at my breasts, massaging them cruelly, while his hot breath tantalised my neck.

Oh, God, it was heaven.

My own fault for adjusting my clothing to look more appealing. I'd left the buttons of my shirt open, worn a sexy black bra that had my breasts almost spilling out and hoisted up my skirt. The reason I didn't have my sexiest panties on was that we'd packed in a rush, not knowing until the last moment that we were being deployed.

'Hey, now, just a minute,' I said, as his hands roamed down again to lift my skirt.

'Shh,' he whispered in my ear.

His fingers pulled my panties midway down my thighs. I quivered in anticipation as he left me like that for a few moments, the cold air caressing my skin before he grabbed my cheeks. He gave them a quick squeeze and I moaned softly, then gasped as he grabbed at the crutch of my panties and tore them right off – not an easy feat, I can tell you. I cried out as the elastic stung my skin but my pussy throbbed happily at this turn of events.

I've let guys I've met at bars maul me so why not allow this gorgeous MP to have his fun? And if he didn't give me a ticket, well, all the better.

'I think I need to do a more thorough search,' he said, his mouth close to my cheek, his tongue just licking at the side of my mouth lightly as he pushed his body into me. Something was probing into my butt and I wasn't sure if it was him or his baton.

I was thrilled beyond belief. This secluded road was turning into an erotic interlude, one I was enjoying very much.

He knelt down behind me and raised my skirt higher. My bare arse cheeks quivered under his scrutiny. Then a hand bunched up my skirt and tucked it into the back of the waistband while the other roamed over my butt.

I gulped as he pried open my cheeks. His fingers probed my puckered hole and then something wet was there. His tongue! He was rimming me. No one had done that to me for such a long time. I held my breath, enjoying what he was doing, and then his finger began to poke about, inching its way in a fraction.

'Lean over further,' he demanded huskily.

I lay over the bonnet, my breasts mashed against the steel, the coldness seeping through my bra to turn my nipples rigid. The motor was still running and like a vibrator it heated up my body, causing it to tingle all over. His finger explored deeper while my pussy contracted. Then a hard slap to each cheek and his finger was gone.

'Right! All seems to be in order there,' he said. 'Turn around.'

I stood blushing before him. I wasn't really embarrassed, just hot. The light from his headlights gave him a slightly sinister look. His eyes flashed before he dropped back to his knees to kneel before me. I stood there, my pussy pulsating as he lifted the front of my skirt high and now tucked that into the front of the waistband.

His fingers found their way over my slit. He rubbed up and down before carefully pulling the folds apart. He slipped a finger in and then another, digging about as though he really was looking for something.

My head fell back, eyes staring up at the sky. Never in my wildest dreams had I envisaged this happening. Tonight was supposed to be a night of sexual exploration with officers from different regiments, all sworn to secrecy, all at the peak of their careers ... all of which made the risk even more appealing, more challenging. But now this ... what if someone else drove past while this was going on? How would it be handled? We'd both be discharged and I'd have to – what? Explain what I was doing there in the first place? Impossible.

My Captain had requested I attend, had given me directions and keys to the jeep. If what we were doing was discovered we'd all be severely reprimanded if not dishonourably discharged.

'Open your legs wider,' the MP demanded.

I did and his fingers sunk in deeper. I tried to balance myself, staggering on my heels as he continued his supposed search. I wanted to lie back on the bonnet, open my legs wide for him and allow him to finger-fuck me while I attacked my own breasts. I was aching to free myself from the rest of my clothing, to be naked and fucking like the whore I felt.

He rose, leaving his fingers inside me and rested part of his body against mine while his breath fanned my face. I leaned back a fraction and he slipped his fingers out to smear my juices over my slit, grazing my clit as he did.

I was breathing hard against him; a soft moan escaped my lips. I was already on the verge of coming. Abruptly he pulled away from me, turned me roughly by the hips and pushed me in the back so my hands shot out to the bonnet to balance myself. Naked from the waist down, I felt the night air kiss my fevered skin as I heard the jingle of his belt being undone and then his zipper coming down.

A hard probing as his knob slipped over the nub of my clit before parting my folds, and then he pushed his rock-hard cock all the way in. I shifted a little, bending forward eagerly, grinding my arse back into him. Thank God I'd worn those high heels; they gave me the advantage.

'Feel anything?' I asked cheekily.

'Nothing suspicious, not yet anyway,' he said with a laugh.

What the fuck was I doing?

He began to pump into me and I peered about, hoping

we wouldn't be disturbed. His hands came forward and he grabbed hold of my breasts, squeezing them through my shirt before ripping it open and pulling it down both arms. He unclipped my bra and my naked breasts fell heavily, swaying against the metal bonnet, the nipples hardening further.

I was almost nude. My breasts were exposed, my skirt now bunched up around my waist like a material belt and my high-heeled shoes left nothing much to the imagination.

'Are you sure this is necessary?' I said, breathless.

'I need to check at a different angle,' he said, pulling out of me and lifting me up to sit on the bonnet. The vibrations from the motor and the rawness of it all stimulated me to the point of orgasm.

My eyes absorbed his face while my tongue ran over my lips, the orgasm causing goose bumps to appear all over me. The headlights shadowed his features, giving him an ominous and menacing appearance, thrilling me even more.

His hands roamed all over my breasts and then his mouth was on me, kissing my flesh, biting down on my nipples before squeezing them cruelly between his fingers.

'I think I need to do another cavity search, just to be on the safe side,' he said, yanking me by the legs and then lifting them over his shoulders so he could play with my puckered hole.

84

'Whatever you think best, officer,' I said, squeezing my own nipples, pulling on them until I cried out in pain.

He munched hard on my clit while his finger explored my hole. It was magic, absolutely fantastic. I came in his mouth as his tongue lapped at my pussy. I've never been so turned on in my life.

Then something cold was probing me. I lifted my torso forward and saw his baton, the cold leather of it nudging at my pussy. I made to pull my legs together, to push him away, but he slapped them open.

'Relax,' he said. 'I'm not going to hurt you.'

Still nervous, I watched him cautiously as the baton slipped further and further inside. He pushed it in and out while his fingers played with my engorged clit. I fell back again, my back arching, my nipples stretching forward as another orgasm ripped through me, causing me to gyrate and beg for more.

Removing the baton, he pulled me by the hips towards him, my pussy leaving wet streaks on the bonnet. I wrapped my legs around his back, my arms around his neck, my heels digging into his butt cheeks as he lifted me to him, impaling me, bouncing me up and down on his magnificent cock.

He fucked me like a man possessed and I clung to him, eager to feel him deep inside me. I pulled at his hair, kissed his mouth hard as my juices swam around his granite-like cock. Perspiration dripped from me onto him.

I struggled to rip open his shirt, the buttons popping open as my fingers quickly found his nipples and pinched them. 'You fucking bitch,' he said, laughing, as he wrestled my hands away.

He threw me back on the bonnet, pried my legs apart and leaned on them. I lay there hungry for him, eager for more. He stared down at me and then up at my face before thrusting his cock deeper and deeper, ramming into me with a desperation I've never seen in any other man. He groped my breasts, squeezing them brutally while sucking a nipple up into his mouth, only to bite down hard on it. I was wild for him, this primal encounter bringing out the animal in me.

The headlights were focused only on us, the background dark and mysterious as we two strangers fucked our brains out. It was as though we were the centre of attention in this outback, this rural land, way down in the south of Australia. A rustling in the underbrush had me looking that way but there was nothing I could see or wanted to. I had only one thing on my mind at the moment and that was enjoying this man and his fantastic cock.

Wrapping my legs hard around his back, I kicked at him, urging him on, eager for him to fuck me harder as his cock pummelled its way in to the hilt, all the way to the base of his shaft, the friction of our pubic areas igniting our passion further. He fucked like a wild boar, sweat now pouring off him as he rammed into me, his balls slapping up against my arse as he pounded me, the bonnet humming deliciously as he did.

My skin burned against the bonnet. My juices dribbled down the crack of my butt. I wanted to suck his cock, feel it fill my mouth as I sucked it deep into my throat, but I didn't want him to stop either.

I hung on as he picked up his tempo, my breasts now jiggling all over the place, my back raw from rubbing against the hot metal, as he fucked me harder than anyone ever has before and then finally exploded, gasping and shuddering, allowing me to fall back on the bonnet as he collapsed across me panting, trying to catch his breath.

He pulled his cock out of my saturated pussy and our juices dribbled out of me as he helped me down, my legs weak and shaking. I fell to my knees and sucked his flaccid cock into my mouth. He tried to push me away, his cock sensitive, but I hung on and before long he was hard again.

I sucked harder, lapping at his balls, enjoying the taste of myself as my juices slid down my throat. He moaned, grabbing my hair, holding my head firm to pump his cock in and out of my mouth. Small rocks dug into my knees as he stiffened, shuddered and then shot his load, hitting the back of my throat, making me gag, before pulling away to spray his come over my arm. I lapped at it like a hungry dog as I tried to suck him back in but he pushed me back and I fell onto the dirty road.

I lay there before him, wild-eyed and still hungry. Ignoring me, he adjusted his clothing, obviously finished with me and ready to leave. I stood and clung to him, wanting more. He removed my arms and slapped my arse, then strode purposefully back to his car. He left me standing there on the side of the road as he flashed his lights and roared off.

I was still in shock over what had happened but quickly came to my senses when I saw two pinpricks of light began to grow quickly up the road. Peering down at my clothing I realised how it would look to someone, my shirt nearly in shreds, my bra dangling, my skirt still scrunched up around my waist, my body red with welts and bruising from our passionate encounter.

I reached across the back seat of my jeep, dragged out my coat and wrapped it around me, just in time to see the other vehicle's indicator show that it was pulling in behind me.

What now? I was blinded by the light.

'Attention!' was all I heard. A familiar voice. It was my Captain.

'Sir.' I saluted, my coat falling open as I stood there stupidly.

'Quite a show you put on there,' he said, and laughed.

'What ... sorry, sir ... I beg your pardon.'

'Exactly the reason I invited you. I knew you wouldn't

be able to resist his charms, and the rest of us –' he motioned with his hand and two car lights switched on as he did '– enjoyed the performance. Now, if you'll remove the coat, there are a few of us who need a good blowjob after witnessing that and then we'll be off to our original rendezvous – if you're up to it, that is?'

'Yes, sir,' I said as I fell to my knees.

He reached into his trousers as the others alighted from their cars. I wondered what else was in store for me tonight.

I've always said joining the army was the best thing I've ever done – although, if you ask some of the guys I've been with, they'll probably tell you I'm good at more than that.

Drawing his cock into my mouth, I peered up as a hand smoothed my hair. It was a Navy General, one I briefly met yesterday when the Captain was dismissing me. He was a tall African-American and I was hoping he'd be hung like a stallion. I wasn't disappointed. As he stroked my hair he flopped his cock out. I lunged for it, going from one to the other, my mind racing – where was the rendezvous point and who else would be there?

As a third guy came up behind me I felt a rush of adrenalin surge through me. I'd need it before tonight was out. The two guys pulled back and the third came forward.

Well, well. It wasn't a guy but a woman. Couldn't

see her features properly but as the guys lifted her skirt and her naked snatch appeared before me I parted her flaps and licked long and hard like a cat, nuzzling into her flesh, breathing in her scent until ordered to stop.

She sat on the front seat, her butt on the edge, her pussy beckoning me.

'Lick me some more,' she demanded. 'Roger, your cock now.'

She must have been used to getting her way. From the corner of my eye the General I'd sucked earlier came forward and pushed me out of the way. I watched as he positioned himself between her thighs and thrust his huge black knob into her pretty pink pussy. I wanted to see more but he was shadowing the light.

She wrapped her thighs around him, her heels digging into his arse as she urged him on. I watched as his butt cheeks clenched and flexed, running my hand over his smooth skin before tickling up and down his crack.

'Enough,' she said. 'Let's get going.'

She sashayed over to her jeep and the General helped me find my clothing, which was strewn all over the place. We left the jeep behind and the Captain and I headed off to complete our mission.

Between The Covers
Elizabeth Coldwell

Gloria didn't set off for the bookshop that day intending to earn herself a spanking. She wore red nylon panties, so sheer as to be almost see-through, but not because of the way they would stretch taut across her bottom cheeks as she wriggled prettily on her punisher's lap. No, she chose them because they were simply the first pair she laid a hand on when she rummaged in her knicker drawer, a slice of toast and honey in her other hand as she munched on a hasty breakfast. Cycling through the city streets, headphones jammed in her ears and music turned up loud as she wobbled her way between the cars that queued at the lights by the university library, she thought of nothing but the evening she had planned with her girlfriends. Cocktails and karaoke at the Glitter Lounge: the perfect tonic after eight tedious hours surrounded by books.

91

Like every other morning, she chained her bike to the railings in front of the shop with only minutes to spare before it opened for the day, knocking at the door just as old Mr Weaver was putting the last of the float into the till and preparing to welcome their first customers.

'So glad to see you could join us, Gloria.' He regarded her above the half-moons of his spectacles as he ushered her inside.

She couldn't remember how many times he'd made that exact comment over the years, delivered in the same weary tone, or when she'd first come to decide it was worth risking his wrath, knowing that whatever she did he didn't have the strength to sack her. The man hated confrontation and, although Gloria never did anything to provoke him directly, she knew she had the upper hand in their working relationship.

For the first few months, she'd enjoyed her job, largely because it put a little money in her pocket, letting her enjoy her girls' nights out and the occasional splurge on a saucy pair of panties like the ones she wore today. Still, in those days she'd only regarded it as a temporary post while she looked for something better.

Weaver's was the last independent bookshop in the city, clinging on by its fingernails when others had been swallowed up by the big retail chains. Its success was partly due to its relative proximity to the university, guaranteeing custom from students looking for hard-to-find textbooks and second-hand bargains. It also helped that Marius Weaver genuinely loved books, and was happy to track down out-of-print editions, or take the time to help a shopper unable to choose a suitable book for a relative's birthday.

Somehow, though, his admirable customer relations skills had never rubbed off on Gloria. As the months went by, the realisation dawned on her that, in the present economic climate, the plum job she'd been hoping for wasn't going to come her way and she might well be forced to stock bookshelves for the rest of her working life. Now, her days were spent attempting to see how little work she could get away with while still appearing to be busy. She was sure Weaver knew the game she played, but he'd never questioned her about it directly. And if he did get rid of her, he'd have to employ a replacement, on better terms than the ones she currently enjoyed, and she doubted he could afford that. He'd confided to her on more than one occasion that they were only one hefty rent rise away from going out of business entirely.

Her first indication that today might not fall into her usual pattern of slacking and attempting to avoid any kind of meaningful customer interaction came when a tall, curly-headed individual in a slightly shabby tweed jacket and trousers walked into the shop and exchanged a firm, friendly handshake with Mr Weaver. That in itself wasn't an uncommon sight – people were always coming in to chat to Weaver, many of them academics who'd been placing orders with the shop for years and needed him to find some obscure volume by George Eliot or Baudelaire – but Weaver's reaction to the man's arrival was out of the ordinary.

'Gloria, come over here a moment, would you?' he asked. She put down the towering pile of celebrity cookbooks she'd been holding – carrying books around being an ideal method of convincing anyone looking that she was in the middle of something extremely important and couldn't be interrupted – and did as he requested. 'I'd like you to meet my nephew, Jason.'

Even if he hadn't mentioned that the young man was a blood relative, she'd have seen the resemblance immediately. The sharp bone structure was identical, and they shared the same blue eyes, deep-set and intelligent, though Jason's weren't hidden behind spectacle lenses. Giving him a quick appraisal, Gloria pegged him as a younger, more attractive version of his uncle – in looks, if not personality. When he opened his mouth to say hello, he addressed her in deep Dublin-accented tones that sent a shiver of excitement to her pussy. Irish voices had always been a weakness of hers, and the pitch of Jason's was perfect for ordering a woman to strip and get down on her knees, ready to take his cock in her mouth …

Wondering where that thought had come from, she was startled out of her erotic musings by Mr Weaver. 'Jason's

94

going to be looking after the shop for the next couple of weeks,' he explained. 'I've been overdue a holiday for a while, but I'm also starting to think I need someone to take on the business when I retire. I won't be here for ever, you know –'

'Oh, don't talk about that, Uncle Marius,' Jason chipped in, lips quirked in a smile Gloria found all too appealing. 'They'll have to carry you out of this place when the time comes.'

'Be that as it may,' Weaver continued, 'I'll be spending today showing Jason the ropes, then tomorrow the two of you will be on your own. I'm sure you'll quickly establish the same kind of working relationship that we already share.'

Gloria glanced at Weaver, sensing a rebuke, but his expression was neutral. Had he told Jason how little effort she put into her job? Might he be hoping that, when he returned from his holiday, Jason would have taken the steps to ensure she no longer worked there?

'Well, I'll go and get on with what I was doing before. Lovely to meet you, Jason,' she said, leaving the two men deep in conversation and returning to her stack of cookbooks. The latest culinary TV sensation simpered from the cover, red-glossed lips pouting close to a laden wooden spoon. Food porn for people who can't even boil an egg, Gloria thought dismissively, dumping the pile of books on the display table just inside the front door before scurrying back to the shelves at the back of the shop and hiding herself between Eastern mysticism and alternative healing, where she could happily go unnoticed for an hour or so.

She had other reasons for choosing to lurk here. A couple of years ago, in an attempt to keep up with the bigger chains, Weaver had tried selling coffee and encouraging customers to lounge on an overstuffed sofa, leafing through the latest titles while they drank it. It hadn't made any real difference in terms of sales, and he'd quickly ditched the experiment, but the sofa remained, half-buried in boxes of books. Gloria always found it the work of moments to move enough of those boxes to make herself a little nest, where she liked to curl up with one of the offerings from the bookshop's small, discreet selection of erotica.

Satisfied that she wouldn't be troubled by customers in need of service, Gloria opened the book she'd been working her way through over the last couple of days. It was a collection of female submission stories, several of which were accompanied by deliciously rendered illustrations of naughty girls being bent over laps, kitchen tables and, in one delightful instance, a fallen tree trunk to have their bare bottoms spanked or paddled. Gloria had never been able to express quite why these scenarios turned her on so much; all she knew was that, as she turned the pages, a fresh trickle of her cream seeped into the crotch of her panties, already made damp by spending time in Jason's presence. How would it feel to be one of these girls, manoeuvred into a situation where she couldn't help but submit to a spanking, experiencing a beautiful thrill of shame and humiliation as her panties were slowly edged down, knowing that in moments her exposed cheeks would be bouncing under the impact of a firm palm or wooden-backed hairbrush?

Hardly aware of what she was doing, Gloria sprawled back against the sofa cushions, idly toying with her nipples as she read. They were tight, visible points even through the layers of her blue jersey top and seamless bra, and she thumbed one absent-mindedly as she turned the page, eager to know what punishment would be handed out to the waitress who'd managed to drop a tray of champagne flutes at an exclusive cocktail party. She felt hot between her legs, pussy lips unfurling against the thin crotch of her panties, and surrendered to the growing urge to slip a hand down and relieve the itch.

'That looks like some interesting reading you have there.'

She almost dropped the book in alarm, scrambling into a more elegant sitting position at the sound of Jason's voice, before deciding it might be more expedient to get to her feet and start doing some work for a change.

'I – er ...' Gloria sought for any kind of plausible explanation as to why she might be lying on the sofa, playing with her pussy through her underwear as she devoured the contents of a lurid erotic paperback. What could she say? One look at the cover of the book, and her dishevelled appearance, and Jason would know exactly what state she'd worked herself into when she ought to be out dealing with customers. If it had been Mr Weaver who'd discovered her like this, she might – just might – have been able to talk her way out of it, but she knew there was no bluffing, no pretence where his nephew was concerned. He'd ensure that she lost her job over this, and if she did, she could have no complaints.

'Uncle Marius said you'd most likely be here, with your nose buried in the pages of some dirty book,' Jason continued, smiling. 'Either that, or you'd be in the stockroom, pretending to be looking for something or other. Anywhere but where you're supposed to be, eh?'

So Weaver had known about her hiding place all along. But why hadn't he said anything? He'd had more than enough chances to reprimand her, and chosen not to. Jason's next words helped to make things clear.

'You know how lucky you are to still be here, after everything you've done – or, rather, not done?'

'Yes, and I'm sorry.' Gloria knew she must sound as meek and contrite as the heroine of the story she'd just been reading, but she couldn't help her reaction. Something about Jason's strong, almost brooding presence made her feel vulnerable as well as guilty, exciting her in ways she couldn't explain, and she fidgeted on the spot, anxious to bring the conversation to an end.

'You could have been sacked long before now, missy. From what Uncle Marius says, there are days when you barely do a stroke of work from the moment the shop opens till the moment you leave.'

'So why hasn't he got rid of me, then?' She was genuinely curious by now, as well as defiant.

'Because he knew I intended to take over running the business from him, sooner rather than later. And you just happen to be my favourite type of employee.'

'Really? And what type's that?'

'One who never does as she's told and has managed to earn herself a damn good spanking as a result.'

'Spanking?' Gloria's mouth opened in a small O of disbelief. 'You're joking, aren't you?'

Jason shook his head, taking a step closer to her. When she'd been assessing his body earlier, why hadn't she noticed quite how big and broad he was? He'd shed the down-at-heel jacket he'd arrived in, and with his shirt sleeves rolled up to the elbows Gloria could see all too clearly the powerful contours of his forearms. She sensed those arms could pack quite a wallop in the right circumstances.

'I wish I was, but you can't tell me this hasn't been on the cards for you for quite a while, Gloria.'

'But you can't do this here. Not in the shop. What if someone comes in and sees what's happening?'

'The door's locked, and I've put a sign up saying we'll be back in ten minutes. Though what I'm about to do to you is likely to take longer than that.' Jason's grin betrayed his eagerness to begin. 'There's just one more thing I need before we can get on with your spanking.' Raising his voice, he called, 'Uncle Marius!'

As Weaver rounded the bookshelf and came to join them, Gloria moaned in dismay. 'Oh, please, not him.' Being spanked at all would have been bad enough, but to have her employer as a witness to her humiliation was almost more than she could bear.

'Why not? Don't you think he hasn't dreamed about this moment for a long time, waiting for the day when he'd see you across my knee, suffering the consequences of all your bad behaviour?'

So she was to be put over Jason's knee for this punishment. It might have been the most traditional position of all, but it was also the most intimate. Her body would be pressed tightly against his, and he'd be able to gauge her every reaction as he spanked her, hear every sob – for she would sob, she knew he'd make sure of that.

Jason sat on the sofa Gloria had so recently vacated. Spreading his legs wide to make a suitable platform for her to lie on, he patted the top of his thigh and invited her to join him. For a moment, she hung back.

'I'm waiting, Gloria. You don't want me to make this harder for you than I have to, now do you?'

She shook her head, before tottering on suddenly weak legs to clamber onto his lap. Weaver eyed her with greedy eagerness as she spread herself across Jason's thighs, face down. She turned her face away, not wanting him to see the flush in her cheeks and realise how ashamed she was. Try to deny it as she might, deep down Gloria knew she deserved this punishment. For so long she'd been taking advantage of Weaver's good nature and old-fashioned values, failing to provide him or his customers with a suitable level of service. But that didn't mean he had to stand there, almost drooling, as Jason took the hem of her loose floral skirt and turned it back on itself with slow, precise movements designed to string out the exposure of Gloria's pale thighs.

Jason tucked the bunched-up material into the waistband, and Gloria realised her panties were now on display.

'Oh, very nice,' she heard him murmur. 'Lovely and sheer. Shame you won't have them on for very long, though, isn't it?'

Gloria fought to prevent a whimper slipping from her lips. His words were calculated to humiliate her, but also to arouse. She risked a glimpse at Weaver. In her prone position, her eyes were almost on a level with his crotch, and she couldn't fail to notice the tenting in the front of his baggy corduroy trousers. Jason was hard, too, the heat of his cock evident even through the clothing that separated their bodies.

She'd read about this moment so many times: the calm before the storm of a thorough spanking. Yet for all the breathless descriptions she'd consumed of how it felt, nothing had really prepared her for the moment when Jason's palm made its first connection with her backside. The blow wasn't particularly hard, but still it stung, and she let out a surprised little 'oof!' of pain.

Jason replied in an amused tone, 'This is just the warm-up, Gloria. Save your noise for when things really get going.'

With that, he began to spank her in earnest: swift upward strokes that caused her cheeks to bounce and her body to writhe on the solid shelf of his lap. Again and again his hand fell, covering the whole surface of her cheeks, even finding the sensitive crease where bottom met thigh. Difficult as her punishment was to endure, she soon became aware of a steady heat building in her arse, and lower down, as pain slowly ceded to pleasure and her pussy responded to the unfamiliar stimulation.

'You should see yourself,' Jason commented, pausing for a moment. 'Your bottom's redder than your knickers. Want to take a look, uncle?'

Gloria hid her face as Weaver approached, not wanting to see her employer's reaction. She felt very small, very stupid and very turned on. Even though her bottom burned, she wanted more; needed the embarrassment that would come when her panties were removed.

102

'Oh, that's lovely,' Weaver said, somewhere above her. 'Your bottom really does colour beautifully, Gloria. But I'd get a clearer view if Jason took your knickers off.'

'No, please,' Gloria begged, as Jason reached for her panties, but there was no heat in her protest. She lay, limp and submissive, as he tugged them halfway down her thighs. Her own musk rose to her nostrils. Jason must have noticed it, too, for he chuckled and ran a finger down the seam of her pussy lips.

'You're very wet, Gloria. Obviously you're enjoying this far too much. Maybe we should do something about that.'

When he resumed her spanking, he did so with double the force he'd applied before. She couldn't tell herself she felt the swats more now he'd removed her panties, for in truth they'd been so thin as to offer no protection at all. Their significance had been symbolic: with them off, she couldn't pretend there wasn't something deeply sexual about being ruthlessly bared and spanked by this Irishman who'd been a complete stranger only an hour or so earlier.

The sharp slaps made her writhe more forcefully on his lap. The two men would have a wonderful view of her wet, spread pussy, maybe even the dark whorl of her arsehole as she kicked and yelped, but she'd gone past the point of caring what she looked like. She'd been in need of this spanking for so long, she realised that now; something primal had been unleashed deep within her the

103

moment the blows started to land, and she knew that, once it was over, she'd acquiesce willingly to whatever demands Jason made of her.

He punished her to the point where she began to believe she couldn't take any more. Tears ran down her cheeks and strands of hair were matted to her salt-sticky face, but she no longer cared what she looked like. Any remaining dignity had long since been swept away beneath the tirade of spanks.

Jason slid a finger into her cleft again. This time he lingered there, tracing the soft folds of her lips before homing in on her clit. Using the lightest of touches, he stroked it in swift little circles. For the first time in her life, Gloria appreciated how the network of nerves in her lower body were knitted together, sensation flooding through the whole of her cunt and beyond, feeding on the heat in her punished arse.

A second finger joined the onslaught, sliding up her juicy channel and finding the sensitive spot hidden in her inner walls. He held her steady as she humped back at him, welcoming the intrusion, needing him to push her to her limits and beyond.

'Are you sorry, Gloria?' Jason asked, his voice seeming to come through layers of fog.

'Yes, sir,' Gloria gasped, hardly able to shape the words.

'Will you slack off when you're supposed to be working in future?'

'No, sir.'

'And will you do what you're told for as long as I'm in charge of this bookshop?'

Now her reply came without hesitation. 'Yes, sir.'

'Then come for me. That's a good girl,' Jason crooned, and she obeyed this instruction as she had all the rest, buffeted by the waves of an orgasm so intense it threatened to make her lose her reason, if only for a moment. When he judged she was able to stand he guided her from his lap and used his pocket handkerchief to wipe her eyes. He held her in his arms, and she revelled in his solid masculinity, breathing in fresh sweat and a faint scent of rolling tobacco, feeling herself start to get turned on all over again.

The tender embrace should have been the end of matters, but her erotic reading had told her that would never be the case, not when there were still two erections waiting to be unleashed and satisfied.

'On your knees, Gloria,' Jason instructed her. He made no move to give her panties back.

There could have been customers waiting in the street outside for all any of them knew, but that could wait. Gloria had sunk down to the floor, bare knees coming to rest against the scuffed floorboards, and both Weaver and his nephew had their cocks in their hands, waiting for her oral attention.

This is where I belong, Gloria thought giddily, reaching out to take hold of Jason's long, smooth shaft and feed its tip between her lips. Down on my knees with my arse hot and sore, thanking the man who dished out my punishment for spanking me so well.

As she sucked, growing accustomed to his sharp, briny taste, he discussed her with Weaver just as though she wasn't there. 'What do you think, Uncle Marius? Should we make her stand in the corner with her arse on display? Let customers know what happens when a member of staff is disobedient?'

'Why not?' Weaver replied, and Gloria's stomach gave a jolt as she tried to work out whether the man was serious. 'Even better, let's stick her in the shop window, so anyone passing by can see how well she's been punished. Might bring in a few extra customers.'

They chuckled to themselves, swapping talk of how they could further humiliate their naughty employee while Gloria continued to give her undivided oral attention to Jason's cock. When he pulled out, still very far from coming, she turned to his uncle, wrapping her fingers around his shorter, thicker length and sucking that, too. Who knew what ideas Jason might have planned for keeping her in line while Weaver was away? She suspected her spanking might only be the beginning. But as she used her lips and tongue to give both men the sweetest of pleasure, working them to the point where first Weaver, then Jason anointed her tongue with their creamy seed, she knew that, whatever opinion she'd held about the bookshop until now, turning up for work in the mornings was no longer going to be a chore.

Bodies
Lux Zakari

Owen artfully applied a smear of lipstick to the dead woman's mouth, his grey-eyed gaze flicking to his co-worker. 'What're you reading?'

'Lots of things,' Lisa murmured over the clicking of the Portiboy. She turned a page in the hardcover text propped open near naked, bone-white Mr. Jefferson, whom she was embalming in the basement of Frey and Sons Funeral Home.

'I see that.' Shaking away a strand of blond hair straying behind the lens of his wire-framed glasses, Owen finished painting the woman's lips with the brush. He stood opposite Lisa and picked up a book that had been beside Mr. Jefferson's left thigh. '*A Novice's Guide to Reanimation*.' He glanced at the others, scattered across the countertop around the porcelain sink. '*Revivification: The End is Just the Beginning. The Necronomicon?*' A thick blond brow domed. 'Lisa ... what have you been told about bringing your beach reads to work?'

She bit her lip, unsuccessfully staving off a giggle. 'Never you mind, dearie.' She quickly gathered up the hardbacks and transferred them to her tote bag covered in Escher-esque ink drawings.

'Oh, no, you don't. Patronise the Boss's Son Day was last week. Ergo, I demand you let me in the know.'

'Can't I expand my horizons just a bit?'

'The fact you're expanding those particular horizons while doing a particular job is cause for question.'

Lisa shrugged and rubbed Mr. Jefferson's arms, encouraging the flow of formaldehyde. 'After dating a series of losers, I'm just pondering some possibilities.' When she glanced at Owen, she was treated to his horrified expression and laughed. 'Stop jumping to conclusions and let me explain, OK? Maybe you should fix Mrs. Geismark's make-up while you're at it. She looks whorey.'

'Whorey was her style.' He tossed a photograph of Mrs. Geismark, provided earlier by her sobbing son, at Lisa with a smirk. 'Now quit trying to change the subject.'

'Fine.' Lisa sighed, pausing the massage. 'Last night I went out with Blaine.'

Owen's smile fell away. 'Right. That hot date of yours.' He turned back to Mrs. Geismark and unnecessarily dabbed her mouth with the brush.

'That "hot date" turned out to be one of the worst

yet.' Her mouth pursed, Lisa pumped a primer level on the end of the drain tube, freeing a blood clot into the sink with a plop. 'First, he took me to a rifle range to watch him shoot a handgun for an hour. Then he sneaked me into a shitty movie because he could only afford one ticket, and afterwards he got in a fight with a homeless person because he thought the guy looked at him wrong.'

'Jesus Christ.' Owen laughed. 'Where do you find these clowns?'

'Everywhere! But the point is, on the ride home, I got to thinking about my mom, how she used to tell me never to rely on anyone. She'd say this while fixing the roof, sawing down dead trees, changing flats, what have you. Ever since my dad left, she insisted that if a woman wanted something of any value, she'd have to make it happen herself.'

The bridge of her nose started tingling like it always did when she thought of her mother, warning her of oncoming tears. She took a deep breath, filling her lungs with bravery as she often did to fend off the cheerless, confusing thoughts. 'So, why shouldn't that include the perfect man?'

Owen squinted, his lips twisting in confusion. 'Are you insinuating literally *making* the perfect guy?'

'Why not? Look, my mom always said I didn't need a man. After twenty-six years of dating whiners, horn dogs, speed freaks, mama's boys and, worst of all, musicians,

I'm inclined to agree with her. Still –' She lifted her shoulders, her sadness dissolving into excitement. 'I want one anyway. From what I've read, being in love looks like fun.'

'Yeah, I understand the reasoning, but –'

'Not just any guy will do, of course. He has to be someone who'd prove Mom wrong, if she were still alive. He'd have to be totally awesome, beyond belief. So, obviously, he doesn't exist. Yet.'

'Lisa.' Owen again abandoned Mrs. Geismark to stand before his co-worker, folding his five-foot-eleven frame slightly to look her in the eye. 'What're you gonna do?'

The door swung open as Albert Frey, the home's funeral director, wheeled a rattling gurney into the room. Lurking somewhere in his fifties, he was wearing a freshly pressed suit and whistling a blissful, unrecognisable tune. 'Got another for you guys.' An unapologetic grin blossomed on his face. 'I tell you, this heat wave's the best thing that's ever happened to the area.'

'Your father is far too happy to run a funeral home.' Lisa approached the new arrival with a skip in her step as Albert left, singing opera in gibberish.

'Can you blame the guy? He's been inhaling embalming fluid fumes for twenty-some years.' Owen took over rubbing Mr. Jefferson's appendages and cast a nod at the gurney. 'What've we got?'

Lisa unzipped and peeled away the body bag and

instantly clamped a hand over her mouth to suppress a gasp. Inside the casing lay the ashen body of a wiry man with wavy black hair, a Roman nose and a sensual curve to his mouth. He couldn't have been older than thirty, and even with the autopsy scars he was beautiful.

Death never affected Lisa. Even when her mother died, she'd willed herself not to dissolve with sadness. Despite her many offbeat quirks, she viewed death practically and found humour in its inevitability. It was why her career as a restorative artist so suited her. It was a surprise, then, that seeing this corpse made her want to cry. Her lower lip trembled as she thought of who the man had been. What had he thought about every night before falling asleep? Had he ever really been in love? Who'd hurt him the most during his short life? She would never know. What a horrible waste.

'You know him?' Owen shut off the embalming machine and arrived at her side with a look of concern.

She shook her head slowly, wishing with all her heart she had.

Owen opened the folder that had accompanied the body into the room. 'Chase Malvey, twenty-eight, another heat-stroke victim.' He flipped through the file's contents. 'Check it out, the guy was a Cheesehead. His parents want him dressed in a Packers jersey.'

Chase Malvey. Even his name sounded perfect, like a boy who would've been chosen Prom King in high school. What had he been like back then? Did he get good grades? Had he been a happy child? How had he come to love Green Bay's team so much, to the point of being buried wearing its insignia? Lisa couldn't tear her eyes away from him, a deep dark sense of loss churning inside her.

Owen looked up from the folder and his eyebrows knotted. 'You don't look good.' He grabbed her arm before her knees could give out. 'What's going on?'

'We have to do something.'

'About what?'

'About him. Chase Malvey.' She took a deep breath, savouring the aftermath of saying his name.

'We will. We'll make him look great.'

'No.' She pulled out of Owen's grip. 'We have to save him.'

Owen stared at her for a moment, thousands of questions prevalent in his confused features. After a few moments ticked by, he exploded with laughter. 'What are you even talking about?' His incredulous snorts faded as his gaze darted to Lisa's tote bag, brimming with books that now appeared far too topical. He looked at her again, uncertainty replacing his mirth.

Lisa tapped Chase Malvey on the nose. 'Don't you worry. We'll have you back with us in no time.'

* * *

113

'I wish the author'd skip all the history and get to good stuff already.' Lisa drummed her fingers on the diner tabletop behind the weighty *Risorgimento: The Art of Reawakening*, all but the top of her forehead hidden. 'I've gotta revive Chase Malvey before I'm forced to embalm him.'

Owen groaned, dipping a triangle of his wheat toast in his coffee and taking a bite. 'I can't believe you're still talking about that sick idea of yours.'

'It's not sick, it's ingenious.'

'Hate to tell you, my little ingénue, but yeah, it's sick. Now put away the tome so we can have a dinner break with the weirdness kept at a minimum.'

Frowning, Lisa lowered her book to the empty seat beside her in the booth. 'I'm just playing the hand I was dealt.' She speared a potato cube, her eyes a stormy green. 'If I could create the ideal man out of stone or gold like a Roman god, or follow the Judaeo-Christian format and whip up a man of clay, I'd do it. I'd even make one out of flowers like the Welsh if I could.'

Owen shook his head, his mouth agape. 'You're not seriously thinking this can work, are you?'

'Sure. People can do anything if they put their minds to it.'

He rubbed his forehead then sipped his coffee. He'd never met someone as peculiar as Lisa and doubted he ever would. Privately, he found her oddness one of her

114

most endearing qualities, along with her bird's nest of dirty-blonde hair, her freckled button nose and the explosive, contagious laugh she gave upon hearing something most people would find especially fucked up. But while Lisa had always been eccentric and delighted with the bizarre and macabre during her three years at Frey and Sons, this new situation pushed the limits.

She heaved a sigh. 'So do you have plans to help me with this or not?'

Owen nearly choked on his drink, and the mug landed with a clatter on the table. 'Seriously? Are you high?' He looked around for any potential eavesdroppers as he mopped up the hot liquid with a stack of napkins from the metal dispenser.

'I just thought you might want to. I know you're into science-y things. Maybe you could shed some light on some stuff. I remember you telling me you went through a genetic engineering phase.'

'Yeah, a decade ago, and I'll remind you there's a world of difference between trying to combine a ladybug with a wasp and bringing a corpse back to life just so you can date him.'

'If you say so.'

'I do say so. Didn't you tell me once you dabbled in some wicked witchery? Why not just do a love spell if you're really so desperate?'

'What makes you think I haven't tried one already?

115

Besides, now I recognise that building my background in esoteric matters, however slight, was meant to serve me best in this particular situation.'

'So what then? You'd really rather zombie Chase Malvey than any other live guy on the planet?'

She fixed him with a steely gaze. 'Yes, I think I would.'

'Fine.' He raked his fingers through his longish hair, his frustration escalating. 'Say you're not completely delusional. You actually manage to raise the dead. What if this guy was a total asshole in life and continues with that tradition? What if he had a girlfriend and he beat her up? Or let's take another route and say he's the most perfect guy to ever walk the earth. What if he's not into you?' He took a deep breath. 'Not to mention there's other shit to think about, like the Malveys going into shock, ethics getting questioned, lawsuits being filed, people not knowing if you're Christ or the Antichrist so you're lynched in a mall parking lot ...'

'My God, you're such a worrier.' Lisa rolled her eyes. 'It'll be fine. Shake it off. Pretend this is all a John Hughes movie.'

'If we were in a John Hughes movie, we'd have bras on our heads and be using a doll, not a dead body. This is more *Pet Sematary*.'

'Chase Malvey is not a pet.'

'You seem to think he is.' He finished off his coffee, unable to comprehend why he suddenly felt angry. It's not like her plan would actually work. What would it matter either way? He shrugged his shoulders, shaking the thoughts away. 'I better get back.'

'You're not gonna wait for me?'

'I have to dress Mrs. Geismark. Funeral's in a few hours.' He tossed a few dollars on the table and stepped from the air-conditioned diner into the sweltering heat, wishing he didn't feel so irritated. Between him and Lisa, he had a feeling they were creating a whole new brand of crazy.

* * *

The rest of the evening passed in a silence that annoyed Lisa. Though Owen denied he was annoyed with her, he didn't initiate conversation and her attempts to ignite their usual banter fell flat. She gave up and distracted herself as she dutifully worked on Mr. Jefferson while paging through her books, gleaning bits of information here and there from the heavy, dry material. Why was there no one-page, how-to Internet article on the matter? With Chase Malvey's funeral looming in the not-so-distant future, she didn't have too much time to become an expert – not that she saw that as a problem. Her intent would be strong enough to override all the pesky technical details of the ritual. She'd see to that. She thought how proud her mother would've been of

117

her, taking matters into her own hands. For the second time that day, she experienced the tingling in her nose and again shook off the onslaught of grief in favour of moisturising Mr. Jefferson and fantasising about her and Chase Malvey's beautiful future together.

At 9.30, Owen finished overseeing and straightening up after Mrs. Geismark's funeral upstairs with his father, and returned to the basement still wearing his crisp black suit. He gave the room a once-over then paused in the doorway, looking like he wanted to say something. Lisa didn't feel like asking what that something was. As far as she was concerned, she'd made enough tries to talk to him that night. Finally he said, 'See you tomorrow' and retreated up the stairs.

Now alone, Lisa dropped all pretence of working. Mr. Jefferson could wait until tomorrow. She pushed him into the freezer and wheeled out Chase Malvey's gurney. Then, with nervous hands, she opened the bag. Chase Malvey, of course, looked exactly how she'd left him earlier that afternoon. Dead. Perfect.

She worried her lower lip with her teeth, studying the beautiful boy. Not so much a boy as a man, though – a man who'd had a life she knew nothing about. Maybe Owen was right – what if her plan worked and he was a horrible person? What if the living, breathing Chase Malvey wanted nothing to do with her? She tried to tell herself it wasn't possible, that she was too unique to not love and he would be eternally grateful for giving him the gift of life. But what if?

Now that the time for reanimation loomed, Lisa's want subsided and she no longer felt like practising sacraments. The premise of bringing someone back to life seemed unwieldy, impossible, insane. She turned to the counter, where she'd left open *A Novice's Guide to Reanimation*. Where in the world did she get the idea this experiment would work? People tried their entire lives to cheat death. What made her assume she'd be the one to do it after spending less than twelve hours skimming a few books written by authors who'd no idea themselves?

She rubbed her tired eyes, wishing she could blame her obvious insanity on substance abuse. Something had to be wrong with her.

'How goes it, Dr. Frankenstein?'

A scream ripped through Lisa as she snatched up a nearby scalpel and whirled around. Owen, now casually dressed in cargo pants and a T-shirt, laughed in the doorway, his hands raised in surrender and his eyes sparkling with surprised amusement. She freed a whoosh of air from her lungs and slumped against the counter, experiencing the intoxicating rush of relief. 'I'm gonna kill you for that.'

'Then I hope you really are well versed on raising the dead.'

'Isn't rule one in all funeral homes "never sneak up on anyone"?'

'That's rule eight. Rule one is make sure everyone who's supposed to be dead actually is.' He peered at Chase Malvey. 'Speaking of which, he doesn't look very lively.'

'That's because he isn't, genius.'

'I figured you'd brought him back to life and were riding him into oblivion by now.'

'Owen!' She gave a surprised laugh and reached across Chase Malvey to swat her co-worker on the shoulder. 'Where'd that come from? You never talk sexy.'

'Sometimes I do.' He rubbed where she hit him, grinning.

Smiling, she rolled her eyes and huffed, trying to ignore the heat inexplicably creeping into her cheeks. 'Are you here to stop me from destroying your family's business, the Malveys' sanity and the delicate ethical fabric of the world as we know it?'

He hoisted himself onto the countertop. 'Actually, I'm here under the poor guise of helping when frankly I blame my intrinsic curiosity.'

'OK, you're talking like a dork again.' Now that she had an audience, she felt the pressure to perform miracles, so she turned to the book and thumbed through the pages. 'God, when will this chapter just get to the point?'

'No handy tear-out checklist on ritualistic necromancy?'

'Not yet, but while I'm looking, why don't you make yourself useful and look in the freezer? Maybe you'll find someone sexy in there.'

'First of all, the dead are not like dateable ice-cream flavours. Secondly, the only other body in there besides Mr. Jefferson's is old Mr. Kly. Thirdly, just no, on so many levels.'

'Too bad. We could've conjured up a girlfriend for you and double dated.'

He gave a laugh. 'Sounds awesome. You, me and some rotting corpses, sharing milkshakes at the bowling alley.'

'They won't be rotting if we do this right. You really shouldn't be so judge-y. It's not like you have so many great dates either. I'm just trying to help.'

'Thanks for your concern but I'll restrict my options to the land of the living. Less complicated.' He retrieved a spray bottle of disinfectant from one of the glass cabinets. 'Can I ask a potentially weird question?'

She stiffened. 'If it's "how can you think this'll work?" then –'

'It isn't.' He gave the embalming tables a few spritzes. 'How can just a few bad dates lead a pretty girl to this point?'

Lisa swallowed, a tremor rippling through her at the implication Owen found her attractive. She'd never heard him say anything remotely like that about any girl, even the ones he'd dated. This was an unfamiliar development and, as she tossed a questioning glance in his direction, not entirely unwelcome; she found him nerdy and occasionally awkward, but by no means unattractive, and he humoured her self-admitted eccentricities, which made him all the more appealing. She shook her head, determined not to read into it. 'It's not just a few bad dates. It's an entire life's worth of not connecting with anyone.'

Owen wiped the tables down then looked at Lisa, his eyes serious. 'So? Why this guy? What makes him potentially different?'

'He just is,' she sputtered, a vague panic mounting inside her as she realised she had no answer to Owen's query.

'It just seems unlike you to go out with someone strictly based on looks, and by "go out with" I mean "resurrect from the dead".'

Lisa gritted her teeth. 'Thanks for the insight.'

'If you were going to bring back someone from the dead, I'd figure it'd be your mom. Why Chase Malvey and not her?'

'I don't know!' The howl left her before she could prevent it, and again began the tingling in her nose. This time the sensation bloomed too late, and tears filled her eyes before she could will them back. 'Just shut up, all right?'

'Jesus, Lisa.' The innocent playfulness in Owen's expression immediately morphed into regret and shame as he approached her, swearing. 'I am so sorry. That was fucking stupid of me to say.'

She wanted to tell him it was OK, she forgave him,

but the words came out as a sob. She covered her mouth with a shaking hand, trying and failing to hold back the sadness rushing from her. Her lungs felt small and inadequate, and she sucked in a choppy gulp of air but the breath refused to fill her chest. Shoulders shaking, she felt frozen in her sorrow, which had become no longer avoidable.

Owen wrapped his arms around her weak, tremulous body and engulfed her in a way she never expected anyone, let alone him, would be able to do. She hid her wet face in the cotton of his T-shirt and clung to him, permitting herself to cave in to her long-standing grief. He held her, alternating between mumbling apologies into her hair, squeezing her tighter and cursing himself, reassuring her she was safe with him.

When her tears had ebbed and her breathing evened out, she let out an elongated, wavering sigh and pulled away from Owen enough to risk a glance at him. He looked as devastated as she felt and smoothed a strand of hair from her forehead. 'God, Lisa, I –'

'I'm OK.' Lisa stumbled back from his lingering grasp and wiped her eyes. 'Really.' She leaned against the countertop, not trusting herself to stand on her own. How was it possible to feel so heavy and so light, all at once?

'Hop up.' He patted the nearest metal table. 'I'll take care of Chase Malvey.'

She nodded and he helped her perch on the table before

wheeling Chase Malvey into the freezer. Lisa stared at her knotted fingers and chewed her lips, listening to the screech of the door and the rattle of the gurney. When she heard Owen's footsteps return, she looked up, the intensity of his concerned gaze making her flush beneath the bright fluorescent lighting. Experiencing a sudden need to lighten the mood, she gave a small smile. 'No cosmic bowling with zombies for us, I suppose.' Her voice cracked on the last word.

'Not tonight, anyway.' He ruffled her hair before bracing his arms on either side of her, and she felt an unexpected fresh blush at being so near him, seeing him look so sure of himself, so intent on ensuring her happiness. 'It's just as well. I hear bowling with the undead is kind of lame. They're too preoccupied with eating brains. Plus they always insist on playing with the bumpers up. Where's the challenge in that?'

In spite of the evening, she laughed. 'What losers.'

He grinned in a way that made her feel both giddy and shy. Her gaze dropped to the small distance between them, which wouldn't take long to close. Why did she feel so nervous? This was only Owen. She'd known him for years, yet something sparked between them as it never had during her hundreds of bad dates.

She looked up at him again and found him studying her with an unreadable expression in his eyes, a confusing mix of wavering emotions. Acting on impulse to break the silent awkwardness and satiate her own curiosity, Lisa leaned forward and quickly pressed her lips to his.

Owen released a groan from the back of his throat, surprisingly thrilling her with its intensity, and his hands left the table top to cradle her face, locking her to him. His mouth slanted over hers, unyielding, and Lisa twined her arms around his shoulders, blocking out all inclinations but to taste and feel more of him.

His fingers left her cheeks and dropped down her body to the small of her back then up again, as if he were as consumed as she felt and couldn't stop touching her. Then his kisses slowed, his teeth nipping at her lips in a way that made her tremble, and he drew away, his eyes hazy with need. 'You're not just making out with me because you're emotionally distraught, are you?'

'No.' Again she felt her face heat. 'I'm making out with you because you're turning me on.'

He gave a brief nod. 'I'll take it.'

Then his mouth was on her again, his tongue flickering against hers as he stepped between her slightly parted legs, which opened wider, allowing him to press against her fully. She gasped, feeling his hard-on nudge against her inner thigh. A delicious dizzying sensation spun in her head as the situation slipped further from her control and expectations.

His hands moved to the front of her T-shirt, stroking her breasts through the thin fabric, and she moaned against his lips and pushed herself forward further into his palms. His breath fell warm and fast on her cheek as she fumbled for the hem of his shirt, suddenly desperate to feel his skin. They broke away briefly, giving themselves enough time to yank the cotton over their heads, and Lisa's gaze travelled over the bared top half of his lean body before she reached for him again and drew him closer with a scarcely suppressed sigh.

Owen cupped her breasts, still encased in black lace, and his lips found her neck, alternating between licking and biting. Lisa clung to his naked shoulders, her eyes lolling as she gritted her teeth, doing all she could not to scream. His hands then snaked around her back to the clasp of her bra and undid the fastener with an expertise that surprised a laugh out of her. 'Impressive.'

'What, you think I don't know what I'm doing?' He gave her a sexy boyish grin as he freed her from the confines of the lacy fabric before his tongue found her left nipple.

Lisa gazed up at the ceiling as her fingers tangled in his hair and her legs wrapped around his waist, her ankles locking. Obviously he *did* know what he was doing. She could only imagine what else he could do with his tongue and didn't know if she could stand the wait to find out. Her excitement intensified at knowing sweet, unassuming Owen was the one driving her crazy with want.

When his mouth moved to her right breast, she

dropped her hand to the front of his cargo pants and gripped his cock through the material. His lips left her skin briefly as he sucked in a shuddering breath, a sound that made Lisa tremble. When the hell did he get so sexy?

'Your skin is so soft,' he all but moaned as his hands travelled over her breasts, back and stomach. 'It's ridiculous.'

Lisa had to laugh at his word choice. 'If you want to feel any more of it –' She tugged at the waistband of his pants. 'These need to go.'

Owen cast her a look, as if trying to gauge by her expression just how far this moment would go. Finally, without breaking his gaze, he tossed his glasses on the countertop and began undoing his pants. Lisa followed suit, wriggling out of her jeans and panties and kicking them to the floor, until she was naked on the table and he stood nude in front of her, looking at her like he'd never seen a girl without her clothes before.

His cock reached towards his belly button and Lisa couldn't resist touching it, stroking the smooth shaft up to the velvety head. Owen squeezed his eyes shut, his Adam's apple bobbing as he gulped. The sight of this boy enthralled beneath her hands sent a flood of liquid heat to her core.

She patted the tabletop and he sat beside her, wincing as his bare skin touched the cool metal. Then Lisa swung one leg over him, straddling his waist, and tangled her arms around him, revelling in the feeling of his skin next to hers. A thrill rocketed up her spine as he ran his hands up and down her back and exhaled, a shaky breath sounding more like a whimper, his cock pulsing between them. She pressed herself against him further, knowing he could feel how wet she was, and his mouth dropped to her neck. It was her turn to whimper as he nipped the sensitive skin there. In retaliation, she gripped his cock, the skin stretched tight, and gave him a few firm leisurely strokes that turned his kisses aimless as his breathing picked up.

Unable to take the wait any longer, she grasped his cock and, raising herself slightly, steered it into her centre. Immediately she groaned, her muscles clutching him as she sank on him, experiencing his length slowly, completely. Owen released a whoosh of air, staring as she rose then dropped, pleasuring herself by riding him. His fingertips dug into her waist, an act that would've been painful if she didn't think he felt so fucking good.

She moved faster under his watchful, adoring eye, her hips swivelling. His teeth were buried in his lower lip, where the skin was turning white from the pressure. To sense how close he was made her own climax ever the more imminent.

Owen's hands left her waist in favour of her breasts, his gentle touches there a sharp, exhilarating contrast to her hard, measured movements. A moan tumbled from her lips as his fingers coaxed her nipples to life, sending small tremors through her body. He touched and viewed her as if she were a goddess, something to be cherished. She released another groan. It wouldn't be long now.

Feeling herself spiral to the point of no control, Lisa increased her speed and dropped a hand to her clit. Before she could lose herself in the sensations, Owen replaced her fingers with his own, stroking circles over the tight bundle of nerves. His practised motions sent a round of sparks through her body, and she braced her hands on his shoulders and squeezed her eyes shut, surrendering to the electricity flowing through her body directly to her cunt. Unintelligible mumblings fell from her, escalating in volume and frequency and mirroring Owen's own murmurs. Then she felt the familiar rush of pleasure climb her legs and explode inside her, and she collapsed against Owen, who'd also stiffened and shuddered with a guttural sound.

The clinical, poorly lit room filled with the sound of their gasps and sighs. Lisa rested her damp forehead against Owen's bare shoulder as his hands traced feather-light indiscernible patterns over her spine, soothing her back into reality. When her breathing returned to normal, she lifted her head and gave him a smile to match his. 'Hi.'

'Hey.' He brushed away a strand of wet hair clinging to her face.

Lisa looked around the room, suddenly remembering where they were. 'We're sort of screwed up, aren't we?'

'No kidding. This definitely goes down as the most fucked-up place I've ever had sex.'

'Please. You grew up here. You were probably boning girls down here left and right.'

'As the son of a funeral director? I don't think so.' He kissed her forehead. 'No one's as charmingly psychotic as you.'

'Remind me never to mark you down as a reference.'

'Too bad. After today, I'd write you a glowing recommendation for whatever you wanted.'

She tilted her head and arched an eyebrow. 'Despite my total lapse in reality?'

This time it was his turn to blush. 'Absolutely. I love your total lapses in reality.' Owen cleared his throat and gave a grin that hid his sudden apparent shyness. 'You know, I have to admit – for a minute there, you really had me jealous of a dead guy.' He shook his head, breathing out a laugh. 'Who'd have ever thought?'

Lisa smiled to herself as she hugged him close to her, echoing his sentiments exactly.

The Invisible Woman
Amber Leigh

James was so surprised he almost dropped the bottle of beer from his hand.

He thought Corinne looked like a woman on the verge of orgasm.

It was not, he thought, just any orgasm. She looked to be enjoying the sort of orgasm that provided a thrilling, powerful, gushing explosion of satisfaction. The sort of orgasm that should have had a woman screaming with elation. The sort of orgasm a woman was not expected to enjoy whilst attending the staff summer barbecue hosted at the family home of the CEO from Hudson & Hudson Ltd.

She stood alone, unnoticed and untouched by the chaos going on around her.

She was attractive in an understated fashion, wearing an outfit that seemed designed to blend in with her surroundings. It was, he thought, a perfectly unspectacular ensemble for the firm's annual summer soirée. Corinne's jeans were neither too light nor too dark, but the wash-faded colour of a late summer sky. Her top was fashionable but unremarkable: a shapeless garment that concealed whatever figure she possessed beneath. Her unassuming hair, the light application of make-up and even her round-shouldered posture all suggested she was going to great lengths to avoid being noticed.

But, when his gaze lingered on her, he thought she looked like she was about to explode. He could almost imagine her groaning with the release of satisfaction.

He guessed Corinne was disappointed she hadn't been able to wear camouflage for the party. He would not have been surprised to discover her dressed in clothes that were the same colour and pattern as the Ikea-trendy walls of the Hudson family kitchen. Thinking back to the conversational games he sometimes played in the office, games that usually found favour with Liz and her pseudo-intellectual friends, he figured, if Corinne were given the choice of a super power, she would almost certainly pick invisibility.

That would make her an invisible woman on the verge of orgasm.

The thought struck him as amusing but he couldn't bring himself to chuckle.

Something niggled at the back of his mind.

It was the memory of a long-ago night. An office rumour he had been forced to hear? He struggled to remember and was suddenly sure it had been a conversation where a colleague labelled Corinne as dangerous. They said she was the sort of character you'd find in the black heart of a twisted gothic horror story. They had labelled her a cross between a sexual predator and a vampire.

Corinne is a Machiavellian bitch with a sinister agenda.
He could almost hear the words being spoken. He remembered they had come whilst he was sitting at his desk in his cubicle at the Hudson & Hudson Ltd offices.

James pulled on his beer trying to recall who had been talking about her. From past experience, he knew that alcohol seldom helped improve his memory. But it was the only thing available for him to try.

He failed to get hold of the memories. They remained tantalisingly out of his reach, as though they had been trapped beneath a glass bowl. As though the fingers of his recollection were slipping against their surface but making no real purchase.

It didn't help that Corinne looked nothing like a Machiavellian bitch with a sinister agenda. She was the same Corinne he saw occasionally at work during the week. Corinne who took the corner table in the Hudson & Hudson Ltd cafeteria. Corinne who was oftentimes copied into the wearisome emails that did the rounds in the office, but who never seemed to forward any of the emails herself. She was merely Corinne from accounts, an understated wallflower.

An attractive young woman dressed to unimpress.

She stood in a carefully chosen position in the Hudsons' kitchen. Her back was to the dishwasher and, James thought, it looked like the perfect place to stand and be seen to be at the party while being completely ignored by anyone and everyone else there. In any other location her solitude would have been noticed. Because the Hudsons were such convivial hosts, one of them would have taken the time to chat with her and make sure she enjoyed the ambience of the barbecue.

But Corinne had clearly chosen her location with foresight and care.

The kitchen was busy with the Hudsons' many employees constantly milling through. Cherie Hudson made repeated appearances, snatching hot trays from the oven and transferring the contents to freshly emptied plates. Dennis Hudson occasionally brushed past Corinne, collecting empty beer cans for the recycle bins, fishing fresh four-packs from the fridge or taking sausages and burgers for the barbecue outside. Conversations started in the kitchen. Meetings and greetings erupted around her. Everyone passed through on their way to and from the bathroom. And Corinne stood alone and untouched. She was an island in the milling throng. She was overlooked by everyone and everything, except James.

And, he thought, she looked like she was silently coming her brains out.

She shivered slightly. She was a blade of grass caught in a summer breeze. Colour darkened her throat and décolletage. It was the same blush he saw on Liz's neck and chest when she was close to climax. The ice-cubes in Corinne's highball tinkled with telltale tremors. Her lips parted into a sigh of breathless satisfaction.

She's the kinkiest bitch on the face of the planet.

The words came to him with such clarity it was almost as though they were being whispered in his ear. Not that those words had been whispered. They had been spat with venom.

Seriously, if you want to meet the most depraved bitch ever, you should get to know her. But, as a friend, I wouldn't recommend it.

The words echoed through his mind from some vaguely recollected snippet of gossip. He remembered it had been a drunken night doing overtime. The words had come from an angry voice. The conversation had been a hostile blend of sexual secrets and pained belligerence.

He couldn't remember the details of where and when the exchange had taken place. And he wasn't sure the sentiments could be entirely true. Maybe they'd been discussing a different woman called Corinne? It seemed unlikely. It wasn't as though Corinne was such a commonplace name. Surely, whoever it was who had been talking, they couldn't have been talking about this mousy creature?

She didn't look depraved.

She looked like a poster girl for modesty and decorum. She was trying so hard to blend into her background that James couldn't even imagine her giving a guy a hand job.

His gaze slipped to her hands.

Naked fingers encircled the base of her highball. Her nails were unexpectedly long and tipped with scarlet polish. The dwindling ice-cubes continued to rattle musically against the sides of the glass. Was that how her fingers would look if she decided to wrap her fist around his length?

The thought did little to alleviate his growing arousal. If anything, the hard ache in his loins throbbed with the growing need for release.

In his mind's eye Corinne's fingers were holding his shaft and stroking slowly up and down. The languid motion of her wrist was almost hypnotic with its rhythmic rise and fall. He wondered if she would be the sort who gave a guy's cock a soft squeeze each time her grip reached the swollen end. He didn't think she would be that sort. He still thought she radiated an impression of being chaste and proper and uninterested in anything sexual.

But a part of him hoped she would be that sort.

The idea of Corinne squeezing her fist around the end of his cock made his chest tighten with raw longing.

He chugged another mouthful of beer and tried to will away his growing erection. Just because Corinne looked like she was silently creaming her knickers, it didn't mean he could use that as an excuse to come in his pants.

It struck him that, if Corinne had stood anywhere else in the Hudsons' home, she would have been perceived as an obstacle. A little closer to the fridge and she would have been in Dennis's path. Any closer to the oven and she would have been in Cherie's way. If she had positioned herself nearer to the sink she would have been a nuisance to those who gathered there to rinse plates or clean glasses or share kitchen confidences. If she had stood by the counter, which was overladen with oven-warm savouries, she would have been a hurdle to the greedy. But, in front of the dishwasher, she remained a part of the party while being completely distant from everyone and everything around her.

The blush at her neckline darkened.

Her lower jaw fell open as she released a breathy sigh.

She trembled as though her knees were about give out. He had never seen a fully-dressed woman so close to having a public orgasm. It amazed him that no one else had noticed her obvious throes of ecstasy.

The desire to know more was a sudden, inescapable impulse.

He racked his brains trying to remember what else he'd heard about her. It was difficult to bring anything to the forefront of his mind while he basked in the subtle performance of her climax.

She drew breaths in long, thirsty gulps.

The hand around her highball was a tight fist. Her knuckles turned white with the exertion. Even though her large dark eyes drank in every detail of the room around her, James could see her expression was glassy and distant with pleasure.

She doesn't fuck. She's totally celibate.

It was another fragment from that long-forgotten conversation. The words had been shocking with their brutal finality. No one was supposed to use the word 'fuck' in the office. Not in that context, anyway. It was OK to curse the *fucking* customers, or complain about having *fuck*-all in a wage packet. But it was wrong to use the word *fuck* to discuss sexual intimacy. For James it had been an obscene and unlikely revelation of abstinence.

He found it impossible to believe the statement was true.

Corinne was not so beautiful that she turned heads. But she was certainly attractive. She was comparatively young. And she was married to Tom.

The idea that Corinne didn't fuck was unthinkable.

She doesn't fuck?

He was remembering more of the conversation. His own voice had been strained with incredulity. He suspected the words might also have been slurred from too much alcohol.

What do you mean, she doesn't fuck? Surely, she and Tom must …

She doesn't fuck. They make alternative arrangements.

Those final two words were spoken with air quotes. The details of the conversation were finally coming back to him.

Corinne and her husband Tom were rumoured to have an unusual relationship. She didn't want sex but she allowed Tom to go with any woman he fancied. It was some bastardised style of open marriage. Allegedly, she went out of her way to help her husband find new conquests. She experienced sex vicariously through his adventures.

She gets off from him screwing other women?

They're a pair of depraved bastards. Tom gets to screw his way through every married woman in the neighbour-hood, and he does it all with his wife's consent. Corinne frigs herself senseless whilst he's out fucking someone else. More than that, when he gets home, he tells Corinne all about it and she frigs herself again.

Are you serious?

They're a pair of sick and twisted bastards. Steer clear of them.

How do you know all this?

Why do you think I'm getting a divorce?

Now it came back to him.

It had been the office leaving party for Ricky

Short. Banners had hung from the ceiling fans saying, FAREWELL RICK. It was the last Friday of a winter month and his colleagues in admin had organised an impromptu party to say goodbye to Ricky. The man had lost everything in a single, devastating year. He'd lost his wife. He'd lost his home. He'd lost his job.

It had been an *annus horribilis* of disturbing proportions.

James remembered that Ricky had been a maudlin bastard to begin with but the divorce and subsequent upheaval had turned his usual pessimistic outlook on life into something that went beyond bleak. He spent the night of his leaving party in James's cubicle, sobbing on James's shoulder and ranting about the calculating evil of Tom from marketing and Corinne from accounts.

James didn't recall much about that night.

He had forced himself to drink in an attempt to escape the sharpness of Ricky's vitriol. It didn't surprise him that it had taken so long to remember any details from the ordeal. He had struggled with the ensuing hangover for three days afterwards.

Ricky had been bitter and eager to share the cause of his misery with anyone unfortunate enough to appear vaguely sympathetic and find themselves within earshot. Ricky had perceived James as a sympathetic ear and spent the night berating the couple who he claimed were responsible for his troubles.

He had painted a picture of Corinne as an unconscionable madwoman.

She was the personification of demonic evil. In a particularly poetic bout of description, Ricky had suggested Corinne was acting as a puppeteer and controlling the strings of people's lives.

That image made James think of Corinne's fingers. His gaze dropped back to her hands. He felt the muscles of his face stretch into a smile of lewd appreciation. He could still imagine her grip encircling him. He could still imagine her squeezing the end of his shaft.

His erection stirred again inside his pants.

Apparently, according to Ricky Short, Corinne wore the trousers in that relationship. She told her husband whom to bed, and how, and when. She demanded to hear all the salacious details whilst she slaked her carnal thirst. She was apparently in the constant throes of gusset-strumming pleasure and the true source of her satisfaction came from the humiliation and suffering of others.

On reflection, James realised he didn't miss Ricky Short.

At the time he'd thought the idea was far-fetched and scurrilous. Now, looking at Corinne, he was sure he was remembering the cruel gossip and ignorant rumours of a man desperate to blame someone else for his personal misery. The only thing that made James hesitate to dismiss the stories as complete conjecture was the knowledge that

Corinne was almost certainly wallowing in the throes of bliss at the centre of the work's summer barbecue.

She was having an orgasm.

But that proved nothing.

He'd seen Liz's catalogue of sex toys, and helped her pick out various vibrators and plugs for the occasional games they used to play. It was feasible that Corinne could have a small dildo buzzing inside her pussy while she stood alone at the party. He'd read about devices that were supposed to allow a woman to enjoy her pleasure while she was out and about – away from the bedroom – or wherever it was women had sex nowadays. But he'd never imagined those devices being used by someone as unassuming and unremarkable as Corinne. And, even if she was quietly bringing herself to climax in the middle of a party, that didn't mean there was any truth in Ricky Short's allegations.

The idea that she was enjoying an orgasm made his erection throb.

It was as though he'd managed to capture a secret glimpse into the woman's private sex life. Instead of the guilt that would have come from being a skulking voyeur or peeping Tom, he was being allowed the privilege of seeing her orgasm without having to resort to secrecy, prying or Internet fapping.

He could picture the slender plastic phallus dithering inside the dark wet passage of her sex. It would be transmitting a thousand tingles each second. If someone stood too close they could possibly hear the muffled rattle of its motor. The sensations would be pushing her perpetually closer to the point of no return. He supposed he could see the attraction in such a daring scenario. A private orgasm in a public space must be an incredible thrill. To have that satisfaction in the midst of an office party, whilst surrounded by oblivious colleagues and workmates, struck James as the perfect way for a person to get through the ennui of the Hudsons' annual summer event.

And, if that was what she was doing, it explained why she had gone to such pains to make herself unnoticed. She was savouring the ultimate satisfaction while everyone else whiled their way through the minutiae of the barbecue. If it was a choice between enjoying the pleasure of an illicit orgasm or talking to anyone with whom he normally worked, James knew which option he would pick.

He studied her for a moment longer.

Corinne squeezed her thighs together.

It was a subtle movement that no one else would have noticed. But, because he was watching so intently, James saw that the stiffening of her muscles coincided with her lips parting in a sigh of satisfaction. The enigma she presented made him hungry to know more.

He stepped into the centre of the kitchen, stood in

front of her and flexed a cheerful grin. It took an effort of restraint not to wink.

'Corinne,' he began cheerfully. 'It is Corinne from accounts, isn't it? How are you today?'

For an instant there was wariness in her eyes. When she glanced up to see who had greeted her, James believed she was annoyed that someone had focused on her after she had gone to such extreme lengths to be overlooked.

Annoyed, or frustrated? Had she been bracing herself for a second orgasm? Would she have gone to such lengths for the simple thrill of one climax? Surely she would want to savour multiple orgasms if the option was available?

The suggestion of a scowl vanished before he could be sure it had been there. A politic smile touched her lips.

'James.' Her voice sounded steady. Only the slightest suggestion of breathlessness smudged her tone. 'James from admin, isn't it?'

He nodded.

'It's good to see you,' she told him. Her smile seemed sincere. 'Are you here with Liz?'

'I was,' James admitted.

Just like Corinne and her husband, James and his wife Liz worked for Hudson & Hudson Ltd. The company was the town's largest employer.

'I was here with Liz,' he repeated, looking around. 'Although I'm damned if I know where she's disappeared to. It must be an hour since I last saw her.'

Corinne nodded toward the kitchen door that led to the Hudsons' garden. She tipped her glass in the same direction. 'I think I saw her helping with Dennis's barbecue. Her wine glass was looking a little empty. You could earn Brownie points if you take a drink out to her.'

Unable to stop himself, James glanced toward the kitchen door. Then his gaze scoured the kitchen for wine and glasses. He was about to take a step away from Corinne when the realisation of what had happened struck him.

Impressed, James struggled to contain a smile of admiration.

He had been effectively greeted and dismissed without being given the chance to make a proper conversation. He modified his opinion of Corinne and decided, if she was given a choice of super powers, the woman almost certainly wouldn't choose invisibility. She already possessed that power and was using it to maximum effect.

'I'm sure Liz will be OK at the barbecue,' he told Corinne. 'How're you? What're you up to nowadays?'

Her shrug was a slight gesture.

He watched her face intently, wondering if the movement of her shoulders might add extra pleasure to the rush she was possibly experiencing. Were such movements likely to heighten sensation? Would the shrug of her shoulders make the internal dildo in her pussy buzz faster? Harder? Would it make the plastic phallus touch some unexpected depth or gyrate against a particularly sensitive spot?

Her smile remained composed and inscrutable, telling him nothing.

'Same as always,' she sighed.

James didn't dare press further with that line of enquiry. He knew that Corinne was one of Liz's colleagues in accounts. But the little he knew of her beyond her name came from his wife's gossip, the tidbits he had picked up from meeting her at a couple of previous office-related social functions and the scathing accusations of Ricky Short. James couldn't remember what interests Corinne had outside Hudson & Hudson Ltd or whether she and Tom had children. He didn't want to suffer the embarrassment of saying the wrong thing and exposing his ignorance.

'Is Tom here?'

'He's mingling somewhere.'

The stiltedness of the conversation made him want to walk away. Corinne had already given him the excuse. She had told him where he could find Liz, and he thought that any sane man would go in search of his partner rather than suffer the torment of this gruelling exchange.

But he remained intrigued.

He reasoned that if Corinne was going to such lengths to conceal herself, there must be some part of her personality that was valuable enough to need concealing. And he was also determined to discover if she really was recovering from an orgasm, or possibly desperate to bask in another rush of satisfaction. Perhaps she might even want some assistance in achieving that pleasure.

For an instant he could imagine how that would happen.

Corinne would reach out to grab his wrist. Her fingers would be warm and sticky against his flesh as her grip encircled him. She would pull him close and whisper urgently into his ear, 'I want to come. And you can help me.'

If she said the words, James guessed her breath would be ripe with the scent of climax. He trembled at the idea of her touching him so intimately and demanding his assistance. His stomach folded at the idea of being allowed to possess her naked body.

Corinne studied him coolly.

'Cherie and Dennis have outdone themselves this year,' he tried.

'They always get the best weather.'

'Did you manage to get to their Christmas do? I didn't see you there, did I?'

'It clashed with a prior engagement.'

After speaking with her he was still no nearer to learning if she was close to climax, or if that idea had been born from his fertile imagination and the bitter seeds planted by Ricky Short. He was three beers into the afternoon and wondered if his suspicions came from being slightly squiffy and a little bit horny. But, because Corinne was going to such pains to remain invisible, James tried to build the conversation. He wanted to know more about her and discover whether she had enjoyed a thrill of pleasure in the midst of the dull office party.

'So, tell me,' he began. 'What have you and Tom –'

'Is that Tom?' Corinne asked, speaking over him and glancing behind James's shoulder.

He half-turned but could only see Liz stepping through the doorway.

Liz's gaze darted uneasily around the room. Her expression turned flustered and pink-cheeked when she saw him. Her hair was dishevelled. Her throat and the exposed décolletage above her cleavage were flushed and ruddy. James waved across the room to her, and was about to tell Corinne that he couldn't see Tom, but she was already stepping past him, saying farewell with a mumbled 'Nice talking to you, James. Later!'

He caught a waft of floral perfume, intermingled with a scent that was obscenely reminiscent of sexual arousal.

And then she was gone.

And there was something puzzling about Liz's appearance.

And James began to think, if he wasn't three beers into the party, and hadn't been so distracted by the enigma that was Corinne, he would have a better understanding of what had happened and why it felt as though he had missed something significant.

In Your Dreams
Chrissie Bentley

He was still asleep as I drew back the covers, and still soft when I slipped him into my mouth. I held him there for a moment, acquainting myself with his unique flavour and enjoying his quiescence, the calm before the storm of the erection that I knew would soon be filling my throat. I slipped my hand across his balls, to balance the very base of his shaft, and began to work him with my lips.

Tentatively at first; the idea was not to startle him awake with a sense-shattering orgasm, but to draw him slowly from his sleep, feel him growing harder and heavier on my tongue; and feel, too, the changes that I knew would manifest the moment he awoke and comprehended what was happening.

Guys are so funny about early-morning blowjobs. Some try and kid you that they're still sleeping, as though afraid that awakening will bring an end to their bliss.

Others will startle you with the manic transformation from sleeping babe to rampant sex god. And others just move gently to the music with an appreciative sigh or a gentle caress, enough to inform you they're in the land of the living, but that's all. To be honest, those are my favourite times.

But half the fun lies in wondering. And the other half lies in actually being there. Which, in this case, I most certainly wasn't.

An excited voice, high enough to betray its owner's lack of experience, and loud enough to echo through the building, was almost wetting itself with delight. 'So, what did you do?'

The other, aping the sound of unconcerned cool, but no less fevered for all its pretension, uttered a sound poised midway between a laugh and a bray. 'Oh dude, I flipped her over and I gave the hardest fucking of her life.'

'Man. I wish I had dreams like that.'

More laughter, and then the sound of running water, and the opening of the door. The show was over.

It's astonishing how little privacy you have in modern office buildings. Not privacy in the way you'd expect it at home, where you close your door on the outside world and relax into a bubble of your own blissful design; I mean the little creature comforts that you'd hope would be a given in a civilised society. Things like – oh, I don't know, but how about the ability to go to the rest room that your company shares with four others on the same floor, without overhearing a couple of the mailroom guys in the men's room next door discussing their latest horny fantasies?

Which is bad enough when all you want to do is have a pee and get back to your desk. But it's even worse when you catch the conversation's end, and discover who the object of the fantasy is; the name of the midnight fellatrix who stole into a spotty youth's bedroom and brought him to a pulsating climax with a Blowjob Supreme.

'Yeah, that Bentley woman's hot. But man, she must be old enough to be your mother.' (Ouch.)

'Older chicks are great.' (True.)

'They're experienced, dude.' (True, again.)

'I mean, can you imagine how many cocks that chick has choked on?'(Excuse me? I have never choked on a cock in my life. Gagged a little once or twice, maybe, but choked? Fuck you.)

'She could suck you in and blow you out in bubbles.'(OK, yes. I have done that.)

'Well, I'd certainly give her a night to remember.' And so on and so forth in a similar vein, while I sat on the other side of that wafer-thin dividing wall, hearing every word and with all thoughts of my waiting work now forgotten, blazing with a rage I'd not felt in a long time.

Look, I'm not a prude, and I know how guys talk. Yes, I might even be flattered under the right circumstances.

But extreme youth – and this pair couldn't have been more than twenty, twenty-one (I think they were college interns) – has an arrogance and a braggadocio that have never appealed to me, not even when I was that age myself. And, if I can be arrogant myself for a second, the nights I remember best are always the ones where I pull something unexpected out of the hat. Yeah, like the bubbles.

I was still fuming when I walked back into the office, negotiated my way around the drab grey panels that mark out our so-called workstations and punched my computer keyboard so hard that my screensaver shit itself.

I looked at the emails that hung on my screen. Fuck them. Three first-time authors who were going to receive a warm invitation to submit their book proposals to the publisher I worked for were instead on the end of the most scathing rejection note in the database. The one that basically asks them not to bother us again and next time, please use a word processing program, because nobody writes novels in purple crayon any longer. I knew I'd relent long before the letters were printed and mailed, so no budding careers were really destroyed. But it still felt good to crush their dreams, however fleetingly. Well, I had to take it out on someone.

From across the room, Jenna's Internet radio was playing the Kinks. 'Don't Forget To Dance.' I remembered the song from my college days, and I loved it back then.

Still do, in fact. Except now it was taking the piss. That line about 'a nice bit of old' – yeah, thanks for that, Ray Davies. 'They whisper their remarks one to another … you know that you could be their mother.'

Fuck it. I raised myself up, one knee on my chair, and called across the room. 'Turn it down, Jen, I can't hear myself think.'

Jenna's a sweet kid. Late twenties, fabulous figure, cute as hell and sexy as hell, with the kind of full, sensual hips that could fuck a man dry. Which, according to the weekend updates that she delivers every Monday, is precisely what she does.

So why is it that Beavis and Butthead – sorry, Bradley and Trav – in the mailroom over there don't fantasise about her? Why isn't she the gorgeous goddess whose prowess and experience fills their nights and wet their dreams? I heard her call 'sorry', and there was silence as she slipped her headphones on. I hit 'save' and walked over to her desk, pulled an earpiece away from her skull and apologised.

'It's OK, I'm done now. Do you want to get a coffee?'

She nodded and we walked out into reception, past the bust of our company's illustrious founder and over to the 'refreshment station'. Who comes up with these names? It's a coffee pot, for Christ's sake.

Sheelagh, the receptionist, joined us. 'Have you seen the mailroom guys this morning?'

I wanted to bite my tongue, but didn't wholly succeed. 'Oh, they're probably hanging out in the men's room jerking one another off to their latest nasty fantasies. That's what most boys their age do, isn't it?'

Jenna looked at me. 'Wow, where did that come from? Aren't you the one who delivered the lecture last week about us being more open to submissions from younger writers, before our publication schedule started reading like the obituary column?'

'Young writers, yes. Spotty toads who can't even deliver the mail to the right floor half the time, no.' And, right on cue, the pair of them, Bradley and Trav, wandered nonchalantly down the corridor, pushing a trolley piled high with packages. 'Shall we leave this here?'

'Why?' Jenna shot back. My scorn was obviously contagious. 'Are they going to magically deliver themselves?'

'Well, it's just that you're all out here, so we just thought …'

'I doubt that.' Now Sheelagh was joining in. 'Just deliver the mail to everybody's desks, and stop wasting time. You're late enough as it is.'

OK, it's probably my turn. But I'm going to be a lot nicer about it. 'Ah, don't be so hard on them. They're probably just not getting enough sleep.' Then I laughed. 'Oh, but listen to me. You must think I sound like your mother.' Bradley smirked, Trav blushed deeply, and an idea flashed through my mind. Everybody knows that dreams are harmless, even the really bad ones. But what would happen if you thought that somebody really was messing with your dreams? And, even more intriguingly, what if they genuinely were?

I was back at my desk by the time the trolley had been wheeled to my end of the office and, as Trav – my very own dirty dreamer – pawed through the heap of letters destined for me, I laid my hand on his. 'I meant what I said. You look like you've not had a good night's sleep in days. Bad dreams?'

He shook his head a lot more emphatically than he needed to. 'No, no dreams at all.'

I flashed my most reassuringly maternal smile. 'Well, if you ever want someone to talk to about them, you know where I am.' It so happened that we'd published a book on dream interpretation a couple of years back, and I was the editor on the project. It was a load of absolute rot, targeted wholly at the unicorns, rainbows and granola crowd, with an index of symbolism that had kept me giggling for weeks at its sheer simplemindedness. 'If you dream about a garbage bag, it means you need to take stock of your material ambitions.'

But Trav had no reason to know any of that. 'I've actually done a lot of work in that field,' I continued. 'So just give me a shout.'

'I will. Thanks.' His face now glowing beetroot red, he backed away, almost tumbled over his cart and, when he hooked back up with his partner-in-crime and they disappeared out of the office, I picked up at least one sentence of their conversation. 'Shit, dude, it's like she knows.' And that was the end of that.

Except it wasn't.

It was about a week later, and I was working at my desk when my phone rang. It was Jenna, but even with the receiver jammed against my ear I could barely hear her voice.

'Are you whispering?'

'I'm on my cell in the rest room, and you have to come here right now, really quietly. You are not going to believe this.'

I hit 'save' and went out into the corridor, just as Sheelagh hung up her own phone and rose to follow me. 'Jenna?' I asked. 'Jenna,' she confirmed. 'This had better be good.'

It was. Jenna was in the last stall in the ladies' room, the one that shared its wall with the men's room, with her entire frame contorted by pent-up laughter. She shushed us dramatically. 'It's the mailroom guys. One of them's been having wet dreams, but get this. He's actually scared of them. He thinks some woman's put a spell on him or something, and one night he's going to wake up and find that she's bitten his cock off.'

Ooops. 'Has he said who it is?'

'Not yet.' We were still conversing in whispers. 'Except

I know she's a redhead.' She and Sheelagh both looked at me, but the voices from the other room quickly distracted them. Trav was doing his best to sound assured, but all three of us caught the quaver in his voice. He was genuinely nervous. 'I mean, I'm not complaining. If she bites like she sucks, I'd probably come to death before the bleeding got going.'

We grimaced at one another.

'But it's totally spooky, man. And she said she knows about dreams, what they mean, all that freaky shit. What do I do?'

'Fucked if I know. Don't mix up her mail so much and hope she lifts the spell?' That was Bradley, and again Jenna and Sheelagh looked at me.

'So it's definitely someone in this building. OK, who else has got red hair?'

'There's that guy on the top floor, but I doubt it's him,' I bluffed. 'Or how about that cleaning woman?'

'Hardly. They said she's hot. Sorry, Chrissie, but it looks like it's you.'

'Actually, I know it's me. I'll tell you when we get back in the office. Let's see what else they have to say.' But there was silence now, the show was over and, as we made our way back to our desks, I told Sheelagh and Jenna what had happened before. Which meant, once we'd all got over a renewed fit of laughter, that one witch had suddenly become three.

157

Poor Trav. As he walked in (on time!) with our mail that morning, he had no idea what he was in for.

First there was Sheelagh peeling her lunch banana very slowly as he walked into reception, and then snapping off a mouthful with her teeth as he came closer.

Then there was Jenna looking up from her computer monitor to demand, very loudly, whether it was the Incubus or Succubus that fucked guys to death while they were sleeping.

And finally, there was sweet and thoughtful me, looking deep into his eyes when he arrived at my desk and, my voice rich with crooning sympathy, saying, 'You look terrible, Trav. Are you still having those bad dreams? My offer remains open if you feel you need to talk to someone.'

Poor kid. He booked out of the office so fast that he would never even have heard the laughter he'd left behind.

'OK, what's next?' Sheelagh was sitting on my desk, Jenna was crouching on the floor alongside. 'We've put the fear of God into him, and he's probably never going to enjoy another blowjob for as long as he lives. Now what should we do?'

'Chrissie should ask him out on a date.' That was Sheelagh.

'No way. Besides, I'm already seeing someone.' That was a feeble response, and I knew it. But I meant what I said regardless, and repeated it for emphasis. 'No way.'

'No problem,' Jenna shrugged. 'I'll ask him.'

'And if he accepts?'

'Well, then we'll go out. Anyway,' she said with a laugh, 'they all taste the same in the dark ...' She looked up at us, and must have seen the look of disbelief that certainly crept across Sheelagh's face, and probably cast a shadow over mine as well. 'Just kidding,' she snorted. 'Some are saltier than others.'

Swinging her legs, Sheelagh kicked her playfully. 'And cheesier. Don't forget cheesier.' The three of us pulled the kind of disgusted faces that no boyfriend has ever been permitted to see, but which they've all been the cause of at one time or another. 'Maybe that's his problem,' Jenna snuffled between laughs. 'Too much knob cheese, and the smell's affecting his brain.'

'Well, you'll just have to let us know.' I smiled. 'If you even go through with it.' Which she didn't, and that really was the end of that.

Except, once again, it wasn't.

***

The big difference between giving a guy a blowjob while he's sleeping, and him attempting to return the favour and get one while you're sleeping is, there's no sense of mystery, no moment of wakeful wonderment. How could there be? Either you sleep with your mouth wide open, in which case the intrusion of a plunging penis would cause you to panic and gag, and maybe throw up; or you don't, in which case, there's nothing like the insistent hammering of a helmet against your lips to make you sit bolt upright and demand, 'What the fuck do you think you're doing?'

'Aw baby, I woke you.'

'Of course you woke me ...' I began to say. But my words were swallowed as he pushed them back down my throat with his cock, one hand boldly holding his shaft steady, the other pressing on the back of my head. 'Yeah, that's it. Suck it, baby ... all the way down your throat, you know how much I love that.'

My shoulders shrugged: like you're giving me a choice? He was into me like a train, with my tonsils for buffers, and his hips working like pistons. I grasped the top of his legs, slowing his motion while I scooted down a little. I needed to rest my back against the pillow, even if my head was still crashing hard against the headboard with every stroke he took. Thank goodness I don't have neighbours on that side.

At first, he just pounded me, reacquainting my jaw with his size and his strength, while my saliva glands worked overtime, trying to grease his passage past my lips and tongue. But then he slowed, his movements slick and steady, and I could begin enjoying myself too, releasing my hold on his hips to reach around his ass and clutch his balls with one hand, while the other darted down to my pussy. He was far too preoccupied to even think about me, his entire being concentrated in the seven thick inches that were fucking my face, but that was all right. I can bring myself off a lot quicker if I'm the only one down there, my fingers a flicking blur against my clitoris, while my mouth gaped wide and I gurgled my pleasure.

I wasn't sucking, because you can't, in this position. My tongue was flattened, my jawbone ached, and even breathing became a chore. And an irritation. I just lay there while he did his thing, my entire body consumed by the passion of his motion, and hanging on for that tumultuous moment when he would finally come and his seed slipped down my throat like honey, so sweetly that I had to wonder why there are still girls out there who won't swallow their lover's sperm ... who won't even let him come in their mouth. Because, believe me, on your back with your throat wide open, and your own climax racing down the turnpike towards you, that sudden flash of heat and wet, the cry that accompanies it and the final quivering thrusts ... there's no feeling on earth to compare with it.

Or maybe he was thinking of somebody other than himself, because suddenly he somersaulted, so fast that I wasn't even clear how it happened, and rough hands were pulling my legs apart. There was a satisfied grunt as he angled his cock, another as a helping hand slipped

down to guide him in, and one more as he pushed triumphantly forward, spreading the flesh that clung to his
cock, driving himself balls-deep inside my grateful gash.

I drew my legs up, urging him deeper as I raised my
ass, and groped blindly for a pillow to drag down my
body and under my hips. I wriggled for comfort and he
lunged; I hissed for him to be still for a moment while
I manoeuvred the cushion into place, then grasped my
own ankles and pulled my legs higher.

His hands were flat on either side of my head; looking
up into the darkness, I saw his strong chest rise up above
me, his eyes closed but his expression no less intense for
that. He paused, filling me deeper than I could ever have
imagined, then slowly he commenced his withdrawal,
an agonising ache of emptiness flooding me as his cock
drew further back.

Tip touched lips and he hung there, unmoving; and I
lay still too, barely daring to breathe, and not needing to
either. Time froze around his immobility, and I became
absurdly aware of the ticking of the clock, counting the
tocks as he stretched me to eternity; and then he lunged,
driving the air from my lungs with his force, and jarring
my innards with the strength of his thrust.

I heard myself cry out and I caught his face again,
staring down at me now, his lips parted in a subtle invitation to kiss him, but his expression so fierce that I wanted
that too, to be used as a fuck hole, to be pushed to my

limits and never, ever, besmirch the moment with some-thing so suddenly incongruous as tenderness. I turned my head and bit his wrist, and he jerked away, but kept his balance. So I turned again and bit the other, but this time he was expecting me and a fist wrapped itself in my hair, tugging at my roots with just enough strength that my own hand flew up to ease some of the pressure.

He was still moving deliberately, filling me with a sudden push, then pulling slowly out again to tease his glans at my cunt lips. More than once my hand snaked down involuntarily to grasp him, to prevent him from slipping entirely out, and more than once I marvelled at how rigid he was, how firm and how strong; he held his position and my breath was a whine now, a low keening 'pleeeeeaaaaasssse' that I did not even hear myself hissing until his lips spread wide in a teasing, cruel smile, as if daring me to share with him the rest of the sentence.

Nail me.

Pierce me.

Ram me.

'Fuck me!'

I surprised myself with the fury in my voice, and filed away for future embarrassment the deafening volume of my words. But he listened and he obeyed, dropping down so his weight lay on elbows and palms as his hips began to pound and his cock began to slam me, faster and faster, harder and harder. Or were those my commands as my flesh began to tense and the nerve-ends bundled greedily, and my hips thrust back as though my clit were a cock, and I was fucking him with every ounce of strength in my body, pleading in my mind for him to hold back from coming for a few moments more, and a few moments more than that because I'm almost there and if you stop now I will never forgive you.

So many things that I wanted to scream but the words couldn't fit because I was screaming already, and he was crying out too, and that was the trigger that my guts had been waiting for. That was the moment when I ran out of words.

I lay there, shocked and shattered. My body ached, my pussy felt hollow. I reached down and touched myself, marvelled at how he had split me so wide and how I was still yawning now. The pillow beneath me was sopping and I pulled it out from beneath me and tossed it onto the floor. The effort of movement disgusted me; I wanted nothing more than to simply lie here forever, as my breathing slipped back to a motion that did not hurt to contemplate, as my heartbeat stopped ringing like bells in my ears. And I reached out to touch him, but of course he was gone, and I found myself feeling that extra bit grateful that it was Saturday morning, which meant I could lie here all day.

Which meant that I didn't have to get up for work.

Not because I don't want to see anybody today, and

especially not because I've been avoiding the two boys from the mailroom for the past three or four days.

But because, no matter how small an office you work in, and how many vitamins you pop to keep bad things at bay, there's always some insidious little ailment going the rounds of the staff.

Sometimes it's a cold that you just cannot shift. Sometimes the flu, or a stomach bug, maybe.

And sometimes, it's a bout of extraordinarily virulent, and contagious dreaming – the kind of dreams that leave you weak at the knees and wet in the crotch, and aching with lust from every place else.

I wonder if I still have a copy of that stupid dream-interpretation book anywhere round here?

Stud Farm
Deva Shore

With Shania Twain blaring through the radio we drove down the long and dusty driveway to a rodeo that my best friend Sheila had been talking about for ages. Stud Farm ... I giggled at the connotation. A place full of studs ... sounded good to me even if they were just horses. The closest to a horse I'd ever been was one of those mechanical ones you see at some bars.

Sheila had been dying to go to a rodeo all her life. I could think of a million other things I'd enjoy more but she really wanted to go and not on her own. So I thought, why not ... she was always there for me and who knew, maybe it would be fun.

This ranch she'd booked us into was amazing. I was really impressed. There was a huge lake surrounding most of the property. Fenced-off areas held sheep, cattle and horses. We were in Tasmania, way down at the south end of Australia, probably the last place you'd expect a rodeo to be taking place, and this property had to be seen to be believed. It was just like something you'd see on television.

As we pulled up behind a rusty old Holden my eyes focused on a gorgeous arse bending over a motor that was still blowing smoke. Tight grubby jeans spread across his hips, exposing just an inch of his crack. As I opened the door this guy glanced over his shoulder at me and nearly blew me away.

His hair, black and slick, was tied back in a ponytail. One look from those dark smouldering eyes set in his tanned face, and I was lost. He straightened. His torso was naked, rippling with muscles. Perspiration shone on his pecs, and a small trail of chest hair snaked its way downward into an area that bulged with promise. He smirked, giving me the once-over as though I was a piece of prime flesh, horse flesh that is, and I didn't much like it … Who did he think he was? I averted my eyes with a quick flick of my hair and pretended not to see him, feigning interest in my surroundings before climbing up the steps leading to the office. Sheila was nudging me, trying to make eye contact, and I knew she was busting to know if I'd already checked him out.

I rang the bell to alert the owners that we had arrived, and strummed my fingers on the desk.

'Did you see that?' Sheila gushed.

Shh,' I whispered back. 'Not now.'

We waited a while and then impatiently I picked up the bell and rang it again.

The flywire door opened and the guy who'd had his head in the motor sauntered in smiling at us. I ignored him but Sheila couldn't help herself.

'Hi,' she said. 'I'm Sheila and this is Michelle. We're down for the rodeo. I don't suppose you know where the owners are?'

'Probably getting things ready for tomorrow,' he said, shaking her hand. 'I'm Antonio, but everyone calls me Tony.'

Oh, God, he was Latin American. What an accent, sexy, hot and breathy. I could practically feel his breath wash over me. The thought of his lean hard body pressed against my own in a samba or salsa, his hips gyrating, his thigh pushed between my own, had me flushing under his scrutiny.

He held his hand out to me and I shook it reluctantly, embarrassed by my thoughts, gasping as a current ran through me. It was like being zapped by electricity.

I stumbled through an awkward hello while Sheila continued to babble.

Finally he said, 'I can take you to your cabin if you wish. I'll find out which one you're in and leave a note for Amanda. She can come and see you when she's free.'

We followed him along a track and down through

the bush, surrounded by the pungent smell of euca-
lyptus trees and the faint earthy smells of the forest floor.
Kookaburras cried out loudly as we passed, one swooping
close to my head and causing me to duck.

'Don't be frightened of the birds,' he said.

'I'm not,' I snapped back louder than I intended.

Inwardly I was kicking myself for being so immature.
What was wrong with me? I'd never had any problem
with men before. I could handle someone like him back
in the city, so why not here?

'Sorry,' I said. 'I didn't mean to snap.'

'That's cool,' he said, waving off my apology as he
opened the door to our cabin.

He showed us through, mentioning a bush restaurant
was open in the shearing shed. All visitors were welcome.
Sheila thanked him and he left.

'What's the matter with you?' she asked as soon as
the door shut behind him.

'Nothing,' I said. 'He just rubbed me up the wrong
way, that's all.'

'Don't know why. I think he's gorgeous. The way he
speaks and pronounces some of his words. Delicious. I
hope the rest of the guys around here are as good-looking
as him. Oh, look at this view,' she said, pulling aside the
back curtains.

There, spread before us, was the river. Majestic gums
towered overhead, blocking out the sun. We pulled open

the sliding door and breathed in the fresh air. It was brilliant. The cabins were spread far apart, giving us privacy. Perhaps this weekend was going to be better than I thought.

'It is beautiful, isn't it?' I said.

'Gorgeous. Hey, we could go skinny-dipping tonight,' she said, laughing.

'You're really getting into the country way of life. Next thing I know you'll be telling me you want to milk a cow,' I teased.

'Come on,' Sheila begged, 'let's get our suitcases and start exploring before it gets too late.'

We drove our car back the short distance and I noticed more men, rugged in their chaps, vests, cowboy hats and boots. This was beginning to look like a really good idea. The guys tipped their hats towards us, acknowledging our presence and giggling. Sheila and I nodded back, showing we'd noticed them too.

As dusk began to descend we found the shearing shed by the aroma of food wafting over the property. Huge steaks, hamburgers and sausages were being barbecued. A table, sagging under the weight of a mountain of salads, bread, cutlery and desserts, beckoned us. With our stomachs growling we helped ourselves to dinner and looked around for somewhere to sit.

'Hi,' a happy voice said as we sat. 'I'm Amanda. You must be Sheila and Michelle.'

170

'Yes,' I said, shaking her hand. 'You've got a lovely place here.'

'Thanks,' she said. 'Everything in your cabin OK? Did Tony show you around?'

'Yeah, everything's fine,' Sheila said.

'There's an itinerary in your room near the phone listing events, times for meals and just about everything else you need to know. The rodeo begins at eight o'clock sharp tomorrow morning, so it's up to you what you want to do and see.'

'Sounds great,' Sheila enthused.

'If you want to learn any aspect of the rodeo, be it bull lassoing, hog tying, breaking in of horses, or if you want to saddle up a horse and just be on your own, everything is at your disposal. Just find me or Tony and we'll be happy to help you out, OK?'

'That's fantastic,' Sheila said. 'You've got an amazing set-up here.'

'I know. We just love it. Oh, I've got to go and welcome some more guests. Remember, if there's anything we can do just holler, OK?'

'She's lovely, isn't she?' Sheila said.

'Yeah, worse luck. Her and Tony are probably an item,' I said.

'Oh, so now that you know you can't have him you're disappointed, are you?'

I laughed. She was right. There was something about

171

Tony. I couldn't quite put my finger on it but hopefully before the weekend was over I'd find out what it was. In the meantime I scanned the room. The place was packed and everyone seemed to be having a good time.

Another couple sat at our table and we chatted to them for a while. They were from Denmark. Backpackers. They were working on a blueberry farm on the adjoining block. They were exhausted from the hard week they'd put in but promised to catch up with us tomorrow.

As we headed back to our cabin, I spied Tony with a group of men, all talking together. I assumed they were the guys who were in charge of the rodeo and when they looked up we just nodded and kept walking.

'Hmm,' Sheila said as we sat on our porch watching the stars twinkle under a beautifully still night. The neighing of horses and the pungent odour of cattle and earth were relaxing and before long we decided to go to bed in order to get up nice and early the following morning.

Sheila fell asleep immediately but I lay there looking up at the ceiling wondering what it was about Tony that attracted me so. It must have been the fact that he was so different from all the other guys I've ever dated. Guys who wore suits to their jobs, took me out for dinner and dancing, treated me with respect, like a lady.

I envisaged Tony kissing me, one hand groping at my breast, fingers gripping my arse. One thigh would work its way between my legs, knocking them apart. His cock hard against my pelvis, his tongue now on my neck trailing down to my breast.

Listening to Sheila's peaceful breathing, I allowed my hand to steal its way into my panties. I cupped my pussy and slipped a finger inside me. Nice and wet. Hmm, just thinking about Tony had me hot – imagine what it would be like to have him make love to me.

I slipped off my panties, quietly manoeuvred my legs apart and began to masturbate. I'd never done it with someone else in the room with me before and I found it heightened my desire. Within minutes I was coming, stifling a moan that was threatening to escape. I rolled over on my side, hugging myself, dreaming of being broken in by a rough-and-tumble cowboy.

The next day was glorious. We dressed appropriately with jeans, boots and shirts. There was a huge crowd already gathering and buses were ferrying in people. The day was shaping up to be a good one.

I spotted Tony immediately, talking to a group of guys. I thought back to last night, how I'd masturbated thinking about him, and my pussy twitched from the memory. I waved and we kept walking, enjoying the day.

An announcement came over the public address system, calling all women competing in the barrel racing to be at the main arena. I had absolutely no idea what was involved. I thought maybe they ran beside a barrel, rolling it along to see who finished first.

Nothing like it. These women were remarkable. The control they had over their horses as they raced around barrels that were dispersed like an obstacle course was impressive. They were timed to see who could get around the quickest. The horses were practically falling over on their sides, they were so low to the ground.

The girl that actually won was stunning. She wore skintight blue jeans, a denim fringed shirt, hat and boots. Her boots had padding that went way up over her knee. As she swung off the saddle to collect her trophy, she removed her hat and shook out a mane of beautiful red hair. I noticed Tony was right there applauding, whistling as she took a bow.

I felt a pang of jealousy. This was silly; he was nothing to me. I hardly knew him.

We moved on and watched some bareback riding, then steer wrestling and calf roping. I didn't enjoy the calf roping, watching those calves being thrown to the ground then bound, although I did notice my mind wandering off at the thought of being tied up and helpless at the mercy of someone like Tony.

The main event was coming up. Bull riding. Everyone had a break for lunch so Sheila and I made sure we got good seats right near the gate. I wanted to watch this up close. We saw the bulls in a pen nearby and I was startled at how big and nasty they really were. There was no way I'd ever do anything as dangerous as that.

174

Just before it started I noticed Tony coming our way with another cute guy.

'Having fun, girls?' he asked.

'Yeah, it's been a real eye-opener,' I said, smiling.

He introduced his friend, who was called Bluey, and they stayed with us, explaining the process and what was involved. It required a lot of skill to stay on and not break anything coming off. The clowns were great too, entertaining us in between events.

An elderly couple were looking for seats so we got up and gave them ours. Tony and Bluey led us to the fence line and we had an even better view. At one stage the bull lunged towards us. I backed away in fright, nearly knocking Tony flying. He held me in his arms to steady me and I felt his warm breath on the back of my neck as he laughed.

There was a definite bulge in his jeans and I was determined that before this weekend was over I'd get to ride it. Bluey seemed like a nice guy. He was Australian and had a funny way about him. He used slang a lot, making it difficult for us to follow him. He kept trying to initiate conversation as though he was interested in me. I only had eyes for Tony, though, and when the two guys moved off Sheila motioned to me to walk off with her.

'What are you doing?' she asked.

'What, what do you mean?'

'Bluey. It's obvious he's hot for you. Why are you ignoring him?' she asked.

'I'm not. It's just ...'

'What? You're not interested in the Latin Stallion, are you?'

'I don't know,' I said.

'Bluey's a much better catch. He's cute, with his red hair and freckles,' she said.

'Then why don't you go after him?' I said.

'I think I just might,' she snapped at me.

What was her problem? She wasn't my mother. I was determined to have Tony; no one else could compare to what I saw in him.

For the rest of the day we kept bumping into Bluey so in the end we included him in our plans. He was a nice enough guy but not really my type so when Sheila asked him to take her for a ride I thought I'd go back to the stables and see if I could find Tony.

By six o'clock it was all winding down. There was another huge barbecue on tonight and a bush band was there for dancing. Beer flowed freely and everyone was having a good time. Everyone but me. I couldn't find Tony anywhere and I hadn't seen Sheila for ages either.

I decided to go back to our cabin and freshen up. Sheila had the key so I thought I'd go around the back and use the sliding door as I knew I'd left it open to air out the room. You can imagine my surprise when I spied Sheila lying across Bluey's knee on the couch with only her shirt on.

I ducked back out of view wondering what to do now. I could hear them talking in low voices so I snuck a look through the curtains and saw that Bluey was naked. She'd moved off his lap and was now kneeling between his open thighs. He had one of the biggest cocks I've ever seen. I watched fascinated as Sheila's mouth covered his knob, her lips forced to spread, the girth was so wide.

Who would have thought? I was sorry now that I'd spent so much attention on Tony. If I had known Bluey was hung like that I would have had him for myself. I peeked back in to see Sheila's tongue licking up and down his shaft while her hand pumped him steadily. He peeled her shirt off and, grabbing her round the back of her head, gently disengaged her from his cock and motioned to her to straddle him.

I'd never seen Sheila naked before. Well, not like this. A quick glimpse getting in and out of the shower but never in the middle of fucking. She had an amazing body and I couldn't tear my eyes away as she climbed up onto the couch, one knee on either side of him, before lowering her pussy down.

His cock slipped in easily. How long had they been doing this? Did they come here as soon as they left me or had they really been horse riding? Sheila had her head thrown back, her hair cascading over her shoulders as she moved rhythmically, her breasts jutting forward. Bluey lowered his head to her nipple, sucking it into his mouth, while his other hand crushed her breast.

I wanted to keep watching but more than that I wanted some action of my own. I had to find Tony and fast. I hurried to the barn and saw Amanda. She waved me over and I was relieved to not be left on my own.

'Hi,' she said. 'Did you enjoy the day?'

'Yeah, it was fantastic,' I said. 'I loved it all.'

'Did you have a chance to go for a ride on one of our horses?' she asked.

'No, I didn't,' I said.

'Tony's doing a check on the outer fences. Would you like to go with him?' she said, beckoning him over.

Before he had a chance to say anything she practically threw me at him and taking my hand he led me off to the stables. He'd already saddled his own horse and now grabbed another smaller one from the stall for me. He helped me into the saddle, gave me a quick rundown on riding and then we were off.

It wasn't as hard as I thought it would be and pretty soon I was cantering, my hair flying freely in the wind. It was fantastic. With my thighs hugging the saddle it wasn't long before my pussy became aware of the constant pressure as we rode along. Tony pointed out a few things but I wasn't really interested. What I wanted was what Sheila was having back at our cabin, but how was I going to convey that?

He reined in his horse and mine pulled up beside him. 'Hop off,' he said. 'The sun is just about to set over the lake. It will be breathtaking.'

He helped me down, his hands lingering on my waist longer than necessary. I took the moment and pretended to stumble. He pulled me back towards him and I fell into his broad chest. We stared into each other's eyes and then he was kissing me, his mouth all over mine. I was hungry for him and thrust my tongue into his mouth, kissing him hard.

'Whoa,' he said.

'What?' I whispered into his face. 'You worried about Amanda?'

'Amanda! No, I'm sure my sister's fine,' he said with a laugh.

Sister! She was his sister. Knowing that, I boldly ran my finger down the side of his face and over to his lips. He sucked my finger into his mouth, his tongue rolling around it seductively.

'Hmm,' he said. 'Very tasty.'

I didn't need any more encouragement. I replaced my finger with my tongue and kissed him as my hands fumbled with the buttons of his shirt, undoing them and pulling them down over his arms. Then I was at the buckle of his jeans tugging at his belt before pulling down his zip.

He tore his mouth away from mine, looked down at me for a second and then as quick as a flash he tore my shirt from me. Hearing the material rip startled but excited me and as he fumbled with the back of my bra my hands flew back to his zip and into his jocks.

His cock was rock-hard, like granite. He pulled me away from him.

'Take off your boots,' he demanded.

I did.

'Now peel off those jeans.'

I did that too, and ran my fingers along the top of my g-string. I teased him by lifting it away from me a fraction, allowing him to see a glimpse of my pussy in the darkening light.

He lunged at me, his fingers at the crack of my arse, and with a quick flick he ripped them from me, leaving me quivering and naked before him.

'My boots,' he said. 'Help me get them off.'

Without hesitating I did. In the city there's no way I would have allowed a guy to order me around like this, but here, with him, there was nothing I wouldn't do – he only had to ask.

I tugged at his jeans, pulling them down and his jocks at the same time. His massive cock jutted forward and I fell to my knees and took him into my mouth as he kicked his jeans off his feet. He leaned back against the horse, startling it. It neighed, turned its head towards us for a second and then went back to grazing on the lush grass as though it'd seen it all before.

180

He pulled my mouth away from his cock and placed my back against a tree. The roughness of the trunk scratched my skin. He held both my hands high up over my head, then slowly ran his down them, over my fevered skin, around my breasts, over my hips and down the outside of my thighs as he knelt before me.

He knocked my legs apart and his tongue tentatively flicked out at my pussy.

'Hmm, very nice,' he said. 'Very nice indeed.'

I was quivering with desire, barely able to stand. I wanted his cock in me. I needed to be fucked, but he had other plans. He opened my lips as though they were a flower, and his tongue flickered over my slit, in and around the folds, before nuzzling into my clit. I felt myself swoon as a finger probed me gently.

I grabbed hold of his head and tried to pull him up and away from me but he nuzzled in harder, his tongue now lapping at me as his fingers kneaded my arse. With one quick movement he laid me down on the grass and ran his hands over my body again, before resting on my breasts where he tweaked each nipple, tormenting me before sucking one into his mouth.

I tried to pull him down to me and roll him over on his back but he would have none of it. He lavished kisses upon me until my juices were dripping, then his fingers stole their way inside and as I opened my legs to him his mouth came down to crush mine. With my tongue

181

snaking into his mouth and his fingers exploring me I came in a flood of juices.

Arching my back I screamed with pleasure as my orgasm rocked my body. Now I was wild and with all my strength I pushed him backwards, his cock jutting forward, pointing to the sky. I flew on him, impaling myself on his amazing cock. He laughed as I humped into him, unable to satisfy myself, my hunger insatiable.

'Fuck me, you bastard,' I screamed at him. 'Fuck me harder.'

Holding onto my hips he pummelled me with his cock. I pushed back, his cock probing where no other has ever been. I screamed again and again, punching him, kissing him, unable to satisfy my starving pussy as I came over and over again.

He pulled away from me and I saw his cock glistening in the moonlight, wet from my juices. He held his hand out and lifted me towards him before he mounted his horse. I glimpsed his hairy balls just before they slapped down in the saddle and then he hoisted me up so I was facing him and lowered me down on his cock.

Oh God, with my legs dangling, his cock felt as though it was hitting my lungs. Then he kicked his feet into his horse and we began to gallop. He held me fast by the hips as I bounced upon his mighty cock. Never in my life have I experienced anything so fantastic.

With a full moon to guide us he steered the horse

around the paddock as I screamed into the still night. His mouth attacked my breasts as I smothered him into me. He tore at my nipples as they jiggled before him.

Then he was leaning back, skewering me to him as he came, his face contorted with passion, while the horse now cantered along. Our juices were all over him, smearing the saddle and each other. He never lost his erection and after a few moments we continued with this unabashed sexual lusting.

Later, much later, after dressing, we slowly made our way back. In the stables he helped me down, crushing my body to his as he kissed my neck. I held my shirt together, smiling at the memory of our passionate embrace.

'Perhaps I'll see you down here a bit more often,' he breathed in my ear.

'Whenever you like,' I said, totally in awe but trying to be cool.

We walked back to my cabin, my hand held tightly in his. It wasn't until we arrived there that I remembered Sheila and Bluey. They were skinny-dipping in the lake. Tony eyed me and I him. Seeing a sparkle in his eye I nodded and we peeled off our clothes to join them. Laughing we splashed at each other, enjoying the freedom of no clothing.

We spent the night fucking, sucking and holding each other. Sheila's pussy was amazing and the guys lay back as they watched me devour her. My favourite part was sucking Tony's cock while Bluey fucked me and Sheila was at my breasts. As the sun began to rise I knew there was no place I'd rather be than here, at Stud Farm with these two amazing studs.

What a fantastic weekend it turned out to be.

www.ingramcontent.com/pod-product-compliance
Ingram Content Group UK Ltd.
Pitfield, Milton Keynes, MK11 3LW, UK
UKHW022301180325
456436UK00003B/172

9 780007 553167